THE WOODPECKER MENACE
Stories from an accidentally unseparated island

Ted Olinger

Illustrated by Tweed Meyer

Tessi & Jonathan —
Get ready for the best time
of your lives (and I don't mean
reading this). — Ted O.

Plicata Press

Plicata Press
P.O. Box 32
Gig Harbor, WA 98332
www.plicatapress.com

This is a work of most excellent fiction and therefore any resemblance to actual places, persons living or dead, or alleged events to those depicted herein however compelling is sadly coincidental.

ISBN: 978-0-9848400-3-8
LCCN: 2013931527

Grateful acknowledgement is made to the editors of the following journals who have kindly allowed to be reprinted vastly expanded and markedly improved versions of these original articles:

Key Peninsula News: "Key Nation," "Part of Nature," "The Legend of Ghost Dog."

Upstate House Magazine: "The Woodpecker Menace," "The Good Sport," "Saving a Bee."

THE WOODPECKER MENACE

The leaf I saw
return to the branch
was a butterfly.

Moritake
(1473-1549)

Contents

Victor
Grapeview
Rocky BAY
Vaughn
WAUNA
SR302
McCANE Cove
Glen Cove
STRETCH ISLAND
JARRELLS Cove
Herron ISLAND
Key Center
HENDERSON BAY
CUTT ISLE
KEY Peninsula
VanGeldern Cove
CARR INLET
Horse Head BAY
WHITEMAN Cove
LAKE BAY
CASE INLET
Taylor Bay
Longbranch
Pt. Lucy
PITT ISLAND
PITTS WARF
Fairmont
Fox Island
Devils Head
PAYTON PASSAGE
STILL HARBOR
EAGLE ISLE
ANDERSON ISLAND
THE NARROWS
AMSTERDAM BAY
ORO BAY
TACOMA

Key Nation: An Introduction

It is dawn on the Key Peninsula. I know this because a woodpecker is banging its head against the side of my house. What at first I took to be gunshots or a jackhammer is just a bird declaring his love for his territory, his mate, and our siding. Then comes another explosion: our six-year-old kicking open the bedroom door followed by the daily full-throated inquiry: "IS IT SCHOOL TODAY AGAIN?" He does homework over oatmeal, or under oatmeal, as it were, using the worksheet as a placemat. He fills in blanks and answers simple questions. One directs: "Describe your favorite color."

"RAIN," he writes.

We wait together for the school bus on the side of a road walled in by evergreens. I drink coffee while the boy demonstrates the many uses of pine needles, red ants, and gravel. The bus emerges from a tunnel of trees and snaps open its doors at the same time every day. I salute the bus driver and reset my watch as the boy climbs aboard.

Later I prepare to tutor students at a local school. A disheveled fourth grader finishes eating cold cereal from a plastic bowl and drops into the chair next to me, dragging a book on beetles or dinosaurs or quasars. I decide to be inspirational and joke, "Pull yourself together, man. You look like you slept in your clothes."

"I did sleep in my clothes." His eyes glisten.

Afterwards, I ask the teacher what more I can do to help him and his classmates.

"Stay," she says.

In the afternoon, I sit at a T-Ball game watching a baseball roll unconcerned across an infield while the five- and six-year-old players point at it with enthusiasm and tell each other what to do. It is a game one can appreciate at once but spend a lifetime watching. Every child hits, every child runs, every child scores, just never the same way. It's like reading the same book over and over but finding new journeys to the same ending each time.

On the way home I make a detour for a popular fixture who is hitchhiking. He is a regular at our local watering hole and at our library down the road. I know this because he tells me every time I pick him up.

"They let people check out fifty movies at a time. Fifty! I have to watch the same movie fifty times just to figure out what's going on!"

He leads me down a series of tree-walled gravel roads to the land his family homesteaded. Whenever I drive toward some place new to me on the KP, I wonder whether I will find it. The peninsula is fifteen miles long and only one to five miles wide, but is covered by woods and water and a few crossroad communities of small stores, homes and farms. We are connected, barely, by winding tributary gravel lanes that change names more often than they change direction. One may start out heading south on the Key Pen highway, a respectable two lane blacktop, and turn off onto any number of gravel side roads with legitimate-sounding names like "165th Court East, KP North," before plunging into forest or through naked clear-cuts, over salmon streams and around kettle lakes, up and down berry choked slopes and ravines lost to memory, twisting left and right at street signs that say, "East 165th Court Ave Place West For Now," or, "Died of Measles Drive, KP South," or, "Trespassers Will be Shot, Pickled, and Eaten," only to come to rest at some hidden cove on Puget Sound close to your still inaccessible destination under a sign reading something like "Joe's Bay," which will never appear on any map.

My passenger disembarks at such a spot and lumbers into his garden, shifting an armload of books and videos and bottles. He pulls some plants from the ground and hands them to me. "Golden Beets. Fry 'em up and don't spare the salt."

The outside world occasionally pulls me across the narrow bridge that clings to our peninsula from the mainland, then over a larger span from SeaTac airport to some distant city where houses are built closer together than trees can grow. People point, telling each other what to do. I begin to recall what it was like to live in that world instead of the accidentally unseparated island nation that is the Key Peninsula. I forget the color of rain.

At home in the evening, a neighbor emerges from the brambles with a half empty bottle of homemade wine. "Where's the first half?" I ask. "It was a long walk," he says. We sit on my deck and sample his work. Forty or fifty crows glide like shadows across the twilight sky to their nearby roost, all silent to protect its location. "Crows are notoriously proud and possessive of their home territory," I point out, adroitly.

"So is everyone else on the KP," says my neighbor.

The Woodpecker Menace

It was one of those damp, warmish evenings so common to Puget Sound in spring. I was sitting on the deck of our still new-ish house, only now emerging from my little family's first winter in her. I had been contemplating the mold on the railing over the far edge of a martini glass when I heard what sounded like rapid gunfire.

I sat up somewhat straighter and listened to the booming echo in the surrounding woods—or was it the ringing in my ears? The occasional gunshot on the rural peninsula where we live is not uncommon, especially at cocktail hour, but machine-gunning the gathering dusk seemed a bit much even for our sparsely populated neighborhood.

I heard it again: two or three quick, penetrating bursts. Seemed to be coming from the front of the house, near the road. That's it, I thought. Roadwork. Must be a jack-hammer. I forgot all about it.

Before sunrise the next morning, our three-year-old boy kicked open the bedroom door and announced, "I AM

AWAKE." I heard the jackhammer again. A rapid, relentless pounding that seemed both to be in my head and wrapped around it. Of course, I thought, that's what woke him. Damn early though. I'd speak to the work crew up on the road.

But there was no work crew.

I heard it again that evening. And again. I walked down our long gravel driveway to the road. The sound tore open the evening quiet: BDDDDDDDTH! BDDDDDDDTH! BDDDDDDDTH!

My God, I thought. It's coming from our house!

I crept back up the driveway, concealing myself in the rhododendrons. BDDDDDDDDTH! I slinked behind the house. BDDDDDDDDTH! A bright flash rocketed down from the eaves and smashed into the suet basket hanging on our deck. There it was, a tan and speckled woodpecker, shining orange under the wings, talons sunk deep into the suet, twirling at the end of the basket's chain. It sensed my gawking and turned its evil gaze on me. It took off in a blur and vanished into the tree line, violently beating the air with flashes of banded gold.

Dawn next morning. BDDDDDDTH! BDDDDDDTH! BDDDDTH! The walls pulsated. The windows rattled. Our boy kicked open the door. "WOO'PECKER," he said. We lay there, my wife and boy and I, innocents in the dark, listening to this twelve-inch tall bird produce a sound like all the jackhammers of hell destroying the Devil's driveway.

I crept downstairs and silently opened the back door. BDDDDTH! The very air was rent. I looked up to the eaves. He was near the apex of the roof, below the chimney, attacking a piece of flashing. His evil little head snapped back and forth with military precision. He aimed his beak at some secret confluence of roof, flashing and gutter and BDDDDTH! BDDDDTH! BDDDDTH! The sound it produced was stunning, and it was directly above our three-year-old's room. It seemed an honor, in a way, to be thus embraced by the natural world, as if the arrival of the woodpecker was a sublime gift offered with outstretched arm by the open hand of nature.

Four weeks later, neither my wife nor my son nor I had slept past dawn. Five in the morning. BDDDDDTH! Five in the evening. BDDDDDDDTH! Any time in between. BDDDDDDDDTH! The boy started to have bad dreams. My wife demanded action. I searched for an answer in vain until one evening, while sitting on our deck, a small piece of freshly gouged wooden siding floated down and came to rest near my martini glass. The siege of the woodpecker was no longer just mental torture.

Our nemesis had a name—Northern Flicker (*Colaptes auratus*)—and we were not his first victims. The broad migration range of the flicker spills across North America like so much blood, seeping all the way into the deserts of the southwest down to Central America and even Cuba. The male will "drum," as the rapid fire hammering of his beak is called, to proclaim his territory, but principally he drums to attract a mate. If decibels were any measure of desire, we had one lonely woodpecker on our hands. Once paired, however, flickers are monogamous. Ensconced in their choice locale, they may remain for a decade. They will defend their territory to the death.

Ordinarily, flickers seek out dead trees for nest excavation but ignore the well-seasoned wood of older homes. In the absence of appropriate dead wood, they will readily apply their skills to any structure for "drumming," as the bird books modestly call this 20-beat-per-second head banging. Cedar shingles, metal gutters, roof flashing, antennae, chimney caps, highway signs—all are ripe targets for drumming. And the louder the better, for drumming is not a search for food, it is a declaration: "THIS LAND IS MINE. LOVE ME OR LEAVE IT."

It must be said that the Northern Flicker is not only tough, adaptable and fearless—as anyone who has battled it will admit—it is a keystone species. The cavities it creates provide homes for numerous other animals. It is also, ironically, a mostly terrestrial feeder, scouring the ground for ants and termites and other insects potentially harmful to the very same houses it would happily chisel into oblivion by its hammering. "Ant bird" is one of the two hundred or so monikers that have been hung on this terrible creature since our colonial times. Other attractive handles include: Big Sapsucker, Carpintero, Cotton-back, Golden Winged Woodcock, High Holer, Little Wood Chuck, Pecker Wood, Shadspirit, Yellowhammer and, most fitting of all, the Blackhearted Woodpecker for the heart shaped mark emblazoned on its chest, Superman style.

The books urged us to cover up the damage with an array of anti-woodpecker paraphernalia. We took down our suet baskets and bird feeders, enraging the local jay population. We bought a battery-powered motion detecting plastic owl that turned its head and hooted whenever one of our dogs drew near. More extreme measures, such as attaching mirrors near the damage, applying foul tasting muck or stapling strips of Mylar along the roofline were impractical. Our roof, where the flicker chose to drum, is over thirty feet off the ground and too steep to stand on. The idea of renting an extension ladder long enough to reach it and risk plunging to my death while trying to scare away a bird was laughable. For a while.

By April, blood was in the air. None of our simple tricks had worked. The owl batteries had long since died. Friends who had laughed at our troubles now offered sympathy and firearms. I still resisted the idea of attaching anything to our roof, strictly out of concern for my own safety. I was not going to risk my life staple-gunning plastic ribbons to the gutter. Even if it worked, I'd have to go back up there and rip it all down. Or would I? Would we have to leave it there indefinitely? We needed a better answer.

One of the less helpful sympathy gifts we had received was a stuffed animal version of a Northern Flicker Woodpecker. We were encouraged to "try some voodoo on this guy and see what happens!"

Our son commandeered the toy and incorporated it into the menagerie of stuffed monkeys, bears and other exotics that accompanied him to bed each night. He carefully propped each one up among the pillows at the head of his bed, to watch over him as he slept. "We love you all the time, but now it's time to go to sleep," he intoned, which was exactly what we said to him each night.

As I tucked the boy in and observed the woodpecker in his burrow of pillows, I realized we were going about this

whole thing the wrong way.

What if we welcomed this bird instead of fighting it? What if we installed a woodpecker house on our roof, right at his drumming spot? Perhaps he would move in and stop drumming there?

I went to a local tool store to rent the dreaded extension ladder. The aging owner behind the counter demanded to know what I was about. I found it difficult to say out loud, but admitted that I planned to nail a birdhouse to my roof to keep a woodpecker from hammering my home to pieces. He stared at me. "Is it a Flicker?" he whispered, as if one might be listening. "Had one on ah house ah mine once."

My heart quickened. Here was a survivor of woodpecker battle, full of knowledge to share. "What did you do?"

"Moved."

Somehow I managed to climb the ladder, carrying a two-foot tall, six-by-six inch woodpecker house stuffed full of cedar sawdust (to give the flicker something to excavate), a cordless drill, and a bunch of screws. Cheating death, I installed this new totem, and waited for the silence to begin.

The hammering went on. The woodpecker house failed to attract, discourage, or even interest the woodpecker in any way. It occurred to me that this bird was obviously a veteran of many conflicts with humans. And there was that arresting phrase I'd read: "*Will defend their territory to the death.*" It began to hit home.

I am not ordinarily bloodthirsty and am a sincere believer that nature is best left to its own devices. But after more than two months this living hammer had still not attracted a mate despite its singular, incessant and spectacular hammering. After all, I too am part of the evolutionary circle of life. Sometime in May I decided that if he didn't find a date soon, this woodpecker was going to be selected against.

Like all migratory birds, the Northern Flicker is a protected species. However, the federal government has kindly provided, in its familiar tortured fashion, a process by which one may obtain a permit to kill a woodpecker that is damaging property or driving a young family insane. My years in uniform had made me a competent rifleman—and I have been known to trim lofty tree branches with a shotgun—but I was not eager to start blasting holes in the side of my house to kill a bird. I took the decision seriously. With the grim and disciplined patience appropriate for such a measure, I began the tedious filing and phone calling necessary to obtain the two permits that would become my license to kill.

In June, I was still waiting for my Section 37 form from the Department of Agriculture. The dawn hammering and three-year-old-boy door-kicking-open were by now a way of life. Out of frustration, I had taken to shooting clay pigeons at a local gun club. Even my wife, who will use half a roll of toilet paper to capture a spider and safely deliver it outdoors, demanded bloody justice. To add insult, the flicker had grown bold enough to continue hammering on our roof even while I sat quietly on the deck below, now drinking straight gin and grinding my teeth. That was his mistake, because he gave me my plan.

The suet baskets went back up, the plastic owl was recycled, and we no longer shouted and waved our arms at the roof like the hapless maniacs we had become. We ignored the flicker and, thus, made him feel safe. Our boy now sometimes slept through the predawn hammering, and he missed it. On such mornings he would eagerly step out on the back deck and bellow into the woods, "WOO 'PECKER? WOO'PECKER?" scaring off all wildlife in a hundred yard radius. When the flicker invariably returned, the boy secretly studied him through an empty cardboard tube that served as telescope.

His growing attachment troubled me, for I knew now how it would end. The flicker would hammer as usual in the morning. Our boy would go to preschool. My wife would go to work. The dogs would go to their kennel. I would sit, maybe for hours, hiding in plain sight on the deck with a shotgun and crossword puzzle on my lap.

As I waited for the paperwork, I began to dread its arrival. I was preparing to kill a real animal whose plushy stuffed counterpart had a place on our boy's bed, and perhaps in his heart. The more I contemplated our struggle, the more I began to admire this bird. He was stronger than me, or at least more stubborn. I couldn't beat him without going ballistic, literally, and as the inevitability of his destruction became ever clearer in my mind, I became more and more reluctant to put such an ignominious end to such a pure and honest siege. He might die, but he would still have won.

I explained this feeling to my wife, an educated professional, who said, "They call that 'Stockholm Syndrome.' It happens when hostages identify with their captors."

It was a hot morning in July when I left our kitchen and moved toward the deck, murder as usual on my mind, when my gaze fell upon a flicker perched in an apple tree across the yard. Not just our flicker. One of three sitting there wagging their beaks at each other. My hand went to the door handle and they all disappeared in a burst of drunken golden flapping.

This was too much. What could it mean? They seemed identical, though females are indistinguishable from males but for a few small markings. In the electric shock of the moment, I had not looked for these. They were large birds. More males to challenge our Blackhearted Hammer? Or females to make him their Paris?

And then it was over. There was no more hammering, or drumming, or any sign of our bold and lonely woodpecker. The boy continued to call out for him some mornings, "WOOOO 'PECKER? WOOOO 'PECKER?" He scanned the treetops with his cardboard telescope, and we listened for the telltale tropical "ky-ky-ky-ky-ky" of its call. But the woodpecker was gone.

My gun training stopped, the woodpecker house remained vacant, the jays returned to their dominance of the suet. The boy gave up his morning woodpecker calls. He threw away his cardboard telescope. He no longer kicked open the bedroom door at dawn to climb into our bed.

"Is he dead?" the boy asked one night. I pulled the blankets up over his shoulders. The stuffed woodpecker now shared the pillow.

"No, I don't think so. He probably just found a mate."

"What's a mate?"

"It means he got married."

"Will I have to go away when I get married?"

We seemed to have fallen into a deeper subject and I wasn't sure just what it was. Several answers ran through my head. I chose the simplest.

"No."

He closed his eyes and put his hand over the woodpecker's heart.

I missed his kicking in our door at dawn to climb into our bed. I missed the woodpecker, too, for I could not help drawing a parallel between the bird and the boy. He was intrigued by this animal, by its courage and strength and, perhaps, by its defiance. I could imagine a scenario in our own near future where he might side with a woodpecker, where he might feel drawn to those same indelible head banging woodpecker qualities the bird had displayed in defense of what he wanted, or what he loved. I could imagine that happening because I felt it, too.

And then it was autumn. The few shy alders among our towering evergreens had already turned gold. My martinis gave way to overpriced red wines. I was scrutinizing one of these on the deck, wondering at what age it would be appropriate to compel our boy—now at a robust four—to scrub off the flourishing mold, when the familiar report of avian gunfire erupted overhead. The flicker clung to a corner of the birdhouse I had mounted months before. His shining black eyes drew a fearless bead on mine. That scimitar beak became a blur of locomotion hammering away at his house, claiming it with an explosion of sound and sawdust. His summer migration had become winter return. He had come home.

The Good Sport

Like the first timid flowers of spring, T-Ball season caught us by surprise, smoothly slipping unnoticed into our schedules, our wallets, and our very hopes and dreams for life.

The game was poorly understood in our household, at least by me. Miniature little leaguers weighing in at five- or six-years-old square off against a plastic pylon—the "T"— on which sits a rubber-coated baseball. Each player hacks away at this target until he or she gets a hit, which can be anything from a lazy grounder to a line drive into the dugout. But no matter what happens, everybody hits, everybody runs, every team wins. The only competition that exists, or that is supposed to exist, is within each player against him- or herself.

It didn't start this way. When I took my five-year-old boy to T-Ball tryouts, it was a glowering, gray January morning on a frost-covered baseball field. Even the grass crunching underfoot radiated hostility. About two-dozen preschool and kindergarten-aged children roamed the field in their winter coats like scavenging crows, hopping about, picking at the ground, or at each other, and taking flight when coaches tried to shoo them into position. A cabal of parents on the bench pestered the organizers about who they wanted on what team.

"This is orientation. It's not really a tryout," said one coach, bravely. "We're just gonna sort 'em out. You know, earmark 'em."

And so it begins, I thought.

The children, he said, would take turns at the "T" on home plate, hitting the ball a few times to children on the infield. Their luck at the plate and skill in the field would determine their place on a team, their rank in society, the arc of their lives.

I slouched on the bleachers and prayed for rain.

Our hopeful coaches attempted to station a few players at each base, directing them to take turns fielding any balls that came their way. But with the first hit, everything went into motion. Some players ran toward the ball, screaming, hurling their gloves at it. Some ran to their friends, and hurled their gloves at them. Some hopped or twirled in place, cheering, throwing their gloves in the air. The result was a single massive amoeba of T-Ballers writhing back and forth across the infield, arms and legs flailing, oblivious to the shouted instructions of their selfless coaches or enraged parents.

When it was my son's turn at the "T," he swung several times before connecting with a pleasing metallic *clank*, then flung his bat into the shins of the coach behind him and ran after the ball to get it himself. Another player got there first, and my son burst into tears. He ran to the bleachers like a stricken animal and threw himself on me, begging to be taken home. I was so surprised that at first I wanted to laugh. But these were not the tears shed over a broken toy or a stubbed toe. This was a wound of shame and anger at himself. He would not even let me see his face. Leaving the tryout was all I had been thinking about since arriving, but now it occurred to me this moment might be more important, that this might be the birth of that little voice inside that forever hisses, *You're not good enough.*

A stranger's voice came out of me instead to say, "Just go back out there. It'll be all right." Defying every impulse he must have felt in his little body, he stood up and walked back onto the field like one condemned.

Two months later, Opening Day brings blazing sunlight and clouds of pink apple blossoms engulfing our freshly minted players with bright confetti. Little Leaguers from T-Ballers to teenagers stand in formation on that same benighted baseball field, now lush and dry and warm, struggling to tuck-in knee-length shirt tails before reciting the League Oath in unison. From what I can hear on the sidelines, it's a blend of the Pledge of Allegiance and the Code of the Jedi: "We here stand and swear to always do our best, to always play fair, and to always help others to do the same."

I wonder if they have any sense of what they are promising, or what is being promised to them.

As the season rolls forward, our gangly amoeba of the first day evolves with a rangy discipline. When a ball is hit, however feebly, the hitter flies to first base and stays there whether he's safe or not. Our infielders have learned to strike a classic pose when throwing the ball, stretching backward with one arm while aiming forward with the other, then hurling it away with reckless passion.

There is still no telling where that ball will go. It might bounce off the empty pitcher's mound or go rocketing into the stands. Sometimes it even flies into someone's glove, as if by magic—which is exactly how it is received. The fielder's stunned fear gives way to astonishment and pride: "Look, in my glove, a baseball!" We on the sidelines erupt with joy. And it doesn't matter who makes the play—your kid, my kid, our team, theirs. When a girl pulls on her pink batting gloves and squares up to the plate, we don't care whose team she's on. We join her father when he yells, "Punch it, Cupcake!"

We are thrilled by the clang of aluminum when she sends the ball soaring over second base and into the next diamond, maybe with the bat flying right behind. Cupcake might forget to stop at first base and instead stretch it into a home run, weaving through a conga line of opposing players celebrating her hit, but that's all right. No one goes after the ball anyway, out of respect.

When it's my son who gets that kind of hit, I cannot believe he is the same boy who once wept in my arms after his first at-bat. But that is the beautiful mystery of T-Ball. The drama is not in the outcome. When the T-Ballers are grown and older teams turn our diamonds into outfields, we parents will watch a new game with harder rules and more painful outcomes than any of us now dare imagine. Worst of all, we don't know how it will end.

THE WOODPECKER MENACE

My Anarchist Neighbor

I was behind the wheel of my neighbor's truck spinning doughnuts on my lawn when I realized that I had wasted my life.

The crisis began when I asked to borrow his rototiller. It was, I thought, a harmless request. Our new front lawn was nothing but a wide, sprawling weed bed that tormented my sleep. With spring's ever-gradual arrival, I decided to rip it out and begin again.

"Why don't you see if the neighbor has a rototiller we can borrow?" My wife was determined that at least one of us meet the man at the end of our gravel road. This was just another excuse. In fact, we were his new neighbors.

Our small family had just that winter moved to the rural outcropping in South Puget Sound that is the Key Peninsula, and I had already expended tremendous effort into not meeting the neighbor. I knew by reputation that he had enjoyed a long career on the peninsula as some kind of survivalist logger, trading wood for tobacco, alcohol and ammunition. Well into his 70s, he lived alone in an aging trailer with a detached outhouse and no electricity plunked down in the middle of a large compound patrolled by three Chihuahuas and a flightless cockatiel. The perimeter was a blasted battlefield of wood fragments where he'd hand split massive rounds of timber for decades. The ground was littered with the relics of his trade: axes, wedges, mauls, spools of rusted cable, bent and broken chain hoists, and the carcasses of half a dozen vehicles shrouded in plastic blue tarp. All of this was sprawled under the shadow of an enormous American flag, which he dutifully hoisted every morning, upside down.

"A man like that must own a rototiller," my wife insisted.

But one look at his compound told me all I needed to know. I had seen the man himself occasionally parked on some roadside shoulder, rear doors of his rusting Suburban flung open to display firewood piled to the liner. Leaning against the rear bumper would be a piece of plywood with the words "DRY MAD FIR $100." He would be in the driver's seat, his face in a newspaper and a black fur hat more suited to a Cossack jammed on his head.

He would sometimes get a good look at me, too, his vehicle listing under the weight of wood as he went grinding up our road, his Cossack hat just visible above the steering wheel. If I were outside, he'd hold up a hand in a motionless wave that I took to mean, "Stay where you are," or, "Make no sudden moves." This did not bother me.

Then there were the poems. They appeared mysteriously, left on the shelves of local stores, or nailed into prominent roadside trees. A selection could often be found pinned to the bulletin board of our community center, inviting readers to take a copy. Handwritten in clear, block letters, they drew inspiration from a range of topics but invariably attacked some corrosive political influence on society with a fiery sonnet rhyme scheme.

I did not connect these seditious screeds with our neighbor until I observed him plastering one to a pump at our local gas station, a lonely but important outpost due to its situation on one of the three routes off our peninsula, and therefore a good place to reach a large audience. I recognized at once the distinctive block letters swarming the photocopied page with quatrains of righteous fury. Entitled, "Baby Bush Bombs Baghdad," it began:

> Our president warrior wannabe
> Leading a nation content with its cud
> Surrounded by lying neocon sleaze
> Gets us drunk on oil and blood!

Like all of his work, this too was signed, *Your Anarchist Neighbor.*

"Well," said my wife, "maybe he's got a plow."

On the day I finally swung open the gate guarding his property, he was sitting on a stump in front of his trailer, sharpening the teeth of a blackened saw chain with what looked like a petrified rat's tail. He was surrounded by islands of newspapers and notepads anchored by half empty coffee mugs and the kind of decorative ceramic ash trays once found on every bar in America. Instead of cigarettes, they were full of pencil stubs and exhausted pens.

"Ro-to-till-er." He rolled the word around in his mouth like a piece of rotten meat. "I knew you'd come down here sometime, but I didn't think it'd be for something like that." He gazed unblinking at me from under the furry black battering ram of his Cossack hat.

I could tell at a glance this man had led an eventful life. His gravely voice was a good fit for a face well seasoned by the elements, with many lines orbiting a large nose that looked to have been broken and set badly many times. His legs, his hands and his dogs were all stained with burnt oil and sawdust. An old plaid shirt and jeans hung off his lean, stubby build by way of both fading yellow logger suspenders and thick leather belt, while shoots of wild gray hair stuck out from under his hat. But the eyes in the shadow of that hat shone with a certainty and kindness that gave him an air of nobility. It was something I would later find akin to the hard and regal madronas he sometimes salvaged for firewood. Like them he was tough and slow burning. But once the fire was going, it gave off a lot of heat.

"I am not in possession of a ro-to-till-er at this time," he said with sympathy. "But I believe I can help you."

He recommended the 'Burban. This was that same thirty-year-old, eighteen foot, four wheel drive, solid steel urban assault vehicle masked with rust stains and pine tar in which he patrolled the peninsula looking for trees to fell. It boasted a set of salvaged monster truck tires that would have shamed a tank. He directed me to a stepladder leaning against the passenger side door. "You got to climb up into it through the window. The doors've been stuck since George W. stole Florida."

If there was a connection, he didn't say, but added that the electric windows did not work either.

The broken stump of an ignition key lay in the ashtray. The key's tip was buried deep in the ignition. "Yup, that was Dubya too," he said. "What a day."

I was surprised when the engine roared to life and alarmed when my neighbor climbed through the passenger window after me, first passing in his mug of coffee. "Put the stub back in the ashtray or it'll just fall out."

He didn't use the ashtray anymore, he said, at least not for cigarettes. "Had to quit smoking last year after my heart attack. Then got the swine flu in hospital and pneumonia when I got out. I'll never do that again." He shook his head.

"Do what?"

"Quit smoking."

I inched up the gravel road between our homes and into my yard, maneuvering between large stones that lined the road's edge every few yards. "Careful of those damn rocks," said my neighbor. "They were a bitch to put right the first time."

"What do you mean?"

"My old dad and me lined the lanes around the farm here with rocks we cleared from the fields. It was my Grampa's idea, the bastard. Glacial erratics, they're called. Good name." He scowled at the row of granite stones, each about twice the size of a bowling ball.

"Now, put it in low four, lock up the brakes, then gun it and don't let go."

The vehicle lurched forward like an angry bull at the end of a chain, the massive tires pawing up doormat-sized chunks of soil. I gunned it again and the rear end spun around, sending up more doormats.

"Now that's how we rototill on the Key Peninsula." He drained his coffee.

"Time was, I'd have some bourbon in the 'Burban for a job like this," he said. "But I quit drinking in '73, after I challenged Richard Nixon to a fist fight."

He pointed to the few gray and twisted apple trees behind my house. "I used to climb all these trees of yours, before they set me to picking. They were pretty awful, then. Any good now?"

I admitted the trees seemed to produce nothing but hard green stones that failed to ripen, and that I'd done nothing to help them along.

"Well, you've got to trim them and feed them, and you've got to spray every year. We used sulfur. Killed everything that didn't belong and stained everything that did this golden yellow. Stank all to hell and back but goddamn those trees were beautiful."

Then he asked if I had heard about the bear.

Everyone on the KP knew about the black bears that had been raiding overstuffed bird feeders and unsecured trash cans all spring. He reminded me that a bear had recently barged into The 302, our local tavern.

"The bartender shot it, then he had to call the police to come shoot it some more!"

Another bear had attacked a jogger in rural park land before that. And now he knew there was one near our homes, dining on our early berries. The only animals I'd seen or heard were the stray dogs that commuted up and down the gravel road all day.

"Daw-hugs!" he snorted, stretching an extra syllable out of the word. "It's a goddamn bear." Then his voice went up an octave: "And there it is!"

I caught a glimpse of a shining black shape disappearing into some blackberry vines. It was trailed by a few of the local stray dogs barking like lunatics, albeit from a discreet distance.

I had seen bears in the wild and there was no mistaking that glistening sheen of fur. Seeing one in my yard brought home the images of a bear breaking into an occupied building or mauling a jogger.

My neighbor seemed to share that vision. "Let's go!" Rolling forward attracted the attention of the barking stray dogs, which chased us instead of the bear. I laid on the horn to clear a path, and the engine died.

"Oh, hell!" shouted my neighbor. I turned the broken key in the ignition but nothing happened.

"Honking kills the engine."

"How's that?"

"The wiring's shot and the horn shorts it out! Why do you think the doors don't unlock?"

"I thought that was Bush's fault."

"Well, now we need new fuses." My neighbor eyed the barking strays, all large and part pit bull. He did not appear eager to climb out.

He popped open the glove compartment and shuffled through a bundle of papers. "I used to keep a pistol in here for times like this, but I stopped carrying during the Reagan Regime. I was so mad all the time, 'fraid I'd use it!"

He flipped through two or three dozen pages of that neat block handwriting. "Wrote a poem about that, in fact. I've got it here somewhere."

He read one, and then another, page after page of imperial presidents and the spines they lack; of the corporate baron and toady bureaucrat; of the perverse and the progressive, of economies recessive; of the people's plea for jobs and growth; of the just and the unjust, and the rain that falls on both. Like Dante, he followed the monsters to their den; but more like Quixote, he then fought them with his pen.

The sun was low in the sky and the stray dogs long gone by the time we finished his collection. I wanted a cigarette, though I didn't smoke. I also decided to start drinking, heavily, possibly armed with a pistol. Something suitable for scaring stray dogs.

We decided that the danger had passed and climbed through the passenger window and onto the freshly minted moonscape that had been my dead lawn.

The bear emerged from the blackberries. It was huge, darkly glistening in the evening sun, its tail wagging like a giant metronome.

"What the hell is that?" said my neighbor. As the enormity of our situation hit him, he yelled: "Bad dog! Bad dog! Go home!" It lumbered away, unconcerned.

Lacking cigarettes, liquor, or a handgun, it seemed appropriate to at least invite our neighbor in for more coffee.

"That was a really fat dog," I said.

"Looked like a pregnant sow!" he barked, then stood still in the entryway of our modest home and gazed about as if at some natural wonder. "You know, I've been going by this house for thirty years and I've never been inside."

I spent the rest of that spring slowly dragging the chunks of torn lawn into a compost pile, which my six-year-old son would then drag away for his own use constructing a sodden earth fort. I planted pounds of grass and flowers and sprayed our aging apple trees with something that smelled faintly of rotten eggs. Our neighbor would stick his head out the 'Burban's one open window and inhale deeply of the sulfury breeze.

"Hoo-ah, smells like home!"

Stacks of firewood began to appear in front of our house. There was the odd jar of pickled beets, or a bundle of spinach with bits of mud still warm from his garden. There were newspaper clippings, often punctuated with indignant red arrows or disbelieving question marks. And, always, there were poems.

I made a point of visiting the compound every week or two, usually with my six-year-old in tow. He was mesmerized by the yipping, oil-stained Chihuahuas and the yard full of artifacts from this woodsman's life. If he picked up a branch to throw for the dogs, our neighbor would pronounce: "That's cedar, good for starting." My son would hold up another: "Madrona, which you have to split right after you fell." But when my son would point to a standing tree, our neighbor would reel off something like, "I was thumbing my way home from San Diego after the war when

I picked up this acorn in the redwoods and put it in my pocket 'cause I thought I might need to eat it for my supper someday. But then I made it home, and washed my pants and hung 'em out to dry and never saw them again. Thought a bear ate 'em. Then before you know it there's this sapling wearing my pants. 'Course they eventually split and fell off."

It was hard to read my son's expression as he absorbed these dispatches from a world where bears ate laundry and acorns grew too big for their britches. But he seldom let me visit the compound without being at my side. It dawned on me only later that, growing up with no surviving grandparents, he must have felt some unfamiliar comfort whenever we were in our neighbor's presence.

Our neighbor's grandfather had homesteaded 160 acres here at the end of the nineteenth century and cleared as much timber as he could to farm several large fields before succumbing to tuberculosis during the Great Depression. Our neighbor had grown up working the farm, growing hops and picking apples and berries when he wasn't rolling stones out of the fields. When the Korean War arrived, he walked off the peninsula and joined the army determined never to return. If he was going to do backbreaking work, he decided it would be for himself. Yet, decades later, he had returned to the woods he knew best.

When I asked how that came about, he looked at me hard before answering.

"It was that Monica Lewinsky conundrum," he said. "My God, we put this man in office. Well, it was enough to start me drinking again, I'll just say that."

He showed me a half-built sailboat being consumed by the blackberry vines behind his trailer. Maybe twenty feet long and four or five feet wide, it looked like the decaying wooden skeleton of a misshapen box. "That is what a broken dream looks like," he said. "We were living in Tacoma when my wife threw me out over the drinking. I came back here because there was no other place to go. So I thought, I'll just build myself this little scow, and live on that and fish for my supper. It is a scow, by the way, very simple, and I had all the wood in the world."

"What happened?"

"Life." He dug a couple fingers into his plaid shirt breast pocket, fumbling for cigarettes he no longer carried. Then he looked at me, "Don't let it happen to you."

His family had been selling the farm off in parcels of second or third growth for years, including the plat where our own small house sat surrounded by stands of towering trees. He had managed to hang onto a sliver of the original homestead, working on his boat at the end of the road he'd help build, watching houses and families grow up as trees came down. But much of his former land remained undeveloped, and when we walked through those woods together that last summer, he showed me forgotten pastures of tall grass, the ruins of a hidden fruit drying shed, and the broken ranks of ragged apple trees with branches too warped and tangled to bear any more fruit.

New apples were just beginning to ripen on the old trees behind our house that autumn when our neighbor died. There was to be a viewing at the wake. I assumed I would go alone, but my son refused to let me visit our neighbor this last time without him. He clung to my hand as we entered the outer room of the funeral home and into a crowd of plaid shirts and fur hats, suspenders worn with belts, and coffee mugs filled with things other than coffee. I picked a mug up off the table and a man I knew only by sight edged toward me. He wore a faded Aloha shirt under suspenders topped by an aging tweed jacket, and sported a yellowing beard he hadn't trimmed since, I imagined, the Reagan Regime.

"Guess he went to bed and never woke up." He motioned with his coffee mug to the next room. "Didn't figure him for dyin' in his sleep."

"No, I didn't think we got to do that anymore."

He fixed one of his large gray eyes on me while the other wandered the room. Then he produced an unlabeled bottle from his jacket pocket and tipped some of its contents into my mug.

"Here's lookin' up your old address," he said. He kept his good eye on me for a moment, measuring the effect of his moonshine. It tasted strongly of smoldering corncobs and broken dreams. When I did not go blind or pass out, he gestured to the crowd with his mug. "We talk poetry sometimes, you know, and politics, some of us, at The 302. There's an empty stool now, if you're interested."

In the next room our friend lay alone and uncharacteristically silent. His enormous American flag was on a podium next to him, folded into the traditional triangle. Upon it were his white and blue ribbon Korean War service medals, including the Army Good Conduct award. His face had been shaved closer than it ever was in life, and his Cossack's hat was pulled low over his eyes, as if he were napping. He wore a new plaid flannel shirt under his faded logger's suspenders and in his breast pocket was a fresh notepad and sharpened pencil. My son pointed.

"What's that for?" he whispered.

"So he can keep writing poetry."

"In heaven?"

I hesitated. "Very likely," I said.

When we returned home late in the afternoon, I passed through the house to the backyard to clear my head. I had a vague craving for cigarettes and more moonshine. I sat on the deck and watched a butterfly carried by the breeze over our newly green lawn and into an apple tree. Then I saw someone's arm reach up to touch it. The butterfly drifted and again someone reached up to it.

I crept across the yard until I could make out the movement. A young black bear lay on its back under the low branches, lazily swatting at an apple until it fell. He snapped it up with his snout, ran his tongue around his teeth, and yawned. Then he stretched a paw toward the butterfly floating above him, not swatting, but reaching.

The Legend of Ghost Dog

Halloween on the Key Peninsula comes early and stays late. We do things differently, it's true, but we do them with gusto. The tradition of terrifying our children, of course, is exalted above all else.

We do not trick-or-treat around the neighborhood since, for most of us, there is no neighborhood. Stuck at the far end of isolated gravel lanes, we arrive fully costumed at the local community center. Here we fish treats out of each other's vehicles at "Trunk or Treat"—a long row of decorated cars and pickup trucks enveloped in fog and strobe lights, or lined with severed limbs oozing zombie blood over the much coveted candy within.

We retire with treat-filled bags to a nearby Halloween party. Once there, rather than mundanely carving pumpkins, we hurl them shot-put style into our host's sheep pen where they explode with a wonderful crunchy splattering to the delight of the sheep, who rush in to eat them, and to our children, who demand we throw more.

All pumpkin-hurlers are declared winners by our host, a

sort of wolfman/mummy hybrid who wraps his hairy visage in toilet paper for the occasion. We advance to the next challenge. Our children stick their heads into buckets of ice water to bob for apples they would otherwise never eat, especially today of all days. Meanwhile, parents sample the contents of ugly goblets filled with familiar potions to effect strange transformations.

After enough potion is imbibed, we observe the single tradition that has drifted unsullied over the misty salt waters surrounding our peninsula: we tell ghost stories around a bonfire. Each of us dredges up some spectral experience under the sinister gaze of whatever lurks in the darkness beyond the flames. The stories are usually not our own, and we draw freely from the well of collective memory.

When it is our children's turn, before the glowing embers of flaring marshmallows and melting black licorice, we are surprised to hear that they too can dip into that well. There is some mention of Big Foot and Goat Man, vague threats from distant parts. But they speak as one about their own very real shared terror: the Ghost Dog of Vaughn Elementary School.

According to our second-graders, back in Indian times an evil spirit killed a large dog when it wandered into the ancestral graveyard, which, they swear, is just over the fence by the soccer field. "Teachers found the bones," they assure us. The dog's ghost has roamed that lonely corner of the playground ever since, occasionally growling at wandering preschoolers or thoughtless parents who park on the grass. It has been known to sometimes enter the building. "Even on *pizza* day," they whisper.

We drive home in our old convertible under the broad Hunter's Moon. The car is full of family and borrowed children, all of whom want the top up, citing fears of frostbite and ghost dogs. Unfortunately, I am the designated driver and am therefore punishing them with my oft-repeated policy: top down in dry weather. The aging heater is cranked to high, but produces more noise than heat. I point out the alleged Indian graveyard as we roll by the darkened school, so close to our isolated homes.

"There probably really isn't any ghost dog anyway, really, I bet," says my son. His young friends whom we are conveying eagerly agree. Up front, my wife and I say nothing, unnerving them with our deafening silence.

I do not tell them Ghost Dog is a story attached to every cemetery, moor and country lane in the Western Hemisphere. I am still too fond of the ghosts I grew up with. There was one that lurked under my first bedroom (turned out to be a family of skunks). There were the spirits of Civil War soldiers foraging outside my summer camp cabin (feral pigs). In my first apartment there was the ghost who knocked glasses from their shelves all night (a fat gray squirrel I surprised in the oatmeal one day).

As a responsible parent, I had already been forced to dispatch Santa Claus, the Easter Bunny, and the Tooth Fairy without flinching. Was I really going to continue this massacre of imagination by exorcising Ghost Dog, too?

The looming black trees that line our lonely gravel road are damp with icy dew and brush the sides of the car and the tops of our heads with cold tendrils as we slowly coast down to our drive. Suddenly, a chorus of dogs starts up barking and snarling all around us.

"WHAT IS HAPPENING!" demand the children.

When I don't respond, my alarmed wife bangs the dashboard. "Hey, they asked you a question!"

That I do not know the answer does not stop me from answering. "Oh, it's just a bunch of dogs somewhere, and over here, too," I stammer. There is howling of all sizes from homes up and down the road, but what could have set them off all at once?

"They're just barking at a siren," I pronounce.

"There isn't any siren," says my wife.

But there are two bright green dots shining in the rearview mirror. I hit the brakes. The dots shut off like a switch has been thrown. A sleek body pours down into the middle of the road behind us, then leaps into the trees on the other side. The emptiness glows bright red and still in our brake lights, as if the cougar had never been there.

"Dad! What is it?" I wonder whether a ghost is more dangerous than the truth.

"I think you know," I say.

The screaming does not fully subside until we are locked in the house with every light on, every closet door open, and after every child has called their parents to confirm they are still alive even while Ghost Dog is afoot. They tear the costumes from their bodies like they are on fire and console each other with fistfuls of candy.

"I saw it go by!" says a former vampire.

"I could feel it going by!" says a newly retired super hero.

"I heard it breathing!" says my son, a onetime zombie.

"Ghosts don't breathe," says the reformed vampire.

"They do too. Dad, do ghosts breathe?"

Tomorrow, we will return to training our children to survive the real world. For now, I will let Ghost Dog protect them one more night.

Saving a Bee

My wife and I are lazily refilling battered bird feeders in the backyard when our seven-year-old boy comes running at us with a plastic shovel.

"It's a sick bee!" he bellows.

He presents the shovel, on which sits a disoriented bee. You see this sometimes, bees staggering around on the ground, not flying, not pollinating, just trapped in some kind of bee trance.

"These things happen," I say.

"Let's get it some flowers," he says.

"And some water," my wife says.

This ends badly, I say. To myself.

The bee is installed in a glass mixing bowl on the kitchen counter, complete with flower petals and sugar water.

The boy phones a neighbor classmate we call Bug Master. He comes over instantly and together they spend hours observing the bee and modifying its quarters with grass blades and cotton balls, for comfort.

"We should tell Ms. G.," they conclude.

They explain that Ms. G., their first grade teacher, possesses mysterious knowledge about nature.

"She wears sandals," says Bug Master.

Bug Master was a boon to us. Like so much of the Key Pen, our neighborhood is simply a long gravel road running through trees and fields with a few dwellings of assorted description spaced far apart, and no one close to our boy's age anywhere nearby.

Then, mid-school year, Bug Master moved in with his "Gram," a woman my age who lives on our road, while his mother and someone Gram only ever called Ex-Two "work things out."

The boys spent months surveying every anthill, wasp nest and spider web on the road. With Bug Master's guidance, what started as fear and fascination in our son became the rabid fanaticism of the newly converted.

The boys take their bee problem to the mystical Ms. G the next day. That afternoon, they get off the school bus with Ms. G's personal copy of *All Things Apiary* and a magnifying glass the size of a Frisbee.

Bees all over the world are threatened by disease spreading mites, I am informed. Our boy flips open the book and shows me a page with a map of the world on it. Bug Master holds up a hand in grim warning: "This could be a case of mites."

Back in our kitchen, they observe that the bee seems more active than the previous day, and record this in their notes.

"BEE ALIVE MORE," they write.

They examine the bee's wings through the enormous magnifying glass. "I see a lack of mites," says Bug Master.

The boys have not bothered to cover the mixing bowl since the bee isn't flying. I suggest we leave it by an open window since the bee is improving, just in case it decides to fly home.

This strikes a chord. The book describes the need for bee habitat.

"We should put lots of clover in our lawn, for the bees," says our boy.

"I'll discuss that with Ms. G at your next conference," I say.

"Let's build a bee house," says Bug Master, pointing to an illustration of some bird-feeder-like contraption filled to the brim with what look like cigarettes, but turn out to be cardboard cylinders.

"We can put the bee in it to lay eggs," says Bug Master.

"A habitat for bugamity," I suggest.

"Will you leave them alone," says my wife.

They cut and curl toilet roll tubes and construction paper, re-shaping and re-tasking with yards of packing tape, producing a horrendous monstrosity of cardboard the size of a mailbox that would not survive an hour's rainfall.

After school the next day, my son gets off the bus alone.

"He got called to the office for parent pick up. He didn't get his supplies or anything. Ms. G was mad."

We walk down the road and knock on Gram's door.

"She got back with Ex-Two, and they took him with," says Gram, unsmiling.

"Where?"

"Oregon, they said." Gram sounds doubtful.

Walking back up the road to our house, my son asks when his friend is coming home. I tell him we might see Bug Master over the summer, when or if they visit Gram, or sometime. He says we should take pictures of the bee and pictures of the bee house and other bees living in it and send it to Bug Master. I wonder if that will even be possible.

But when we get home, we find the bee is gone. My son is motionless before the bowl below the kitchen window. "It must've got its strength back and flown off," I say. When he says nothing, I add, "You saved it."

"But where did he go?"

We both head out the backdoor. It is a bright spring afternoon. We see birds hopping on tree branches. We smell cut grass on the breeze. We hear buzzing insects all around. I glance toward the kitchen window and notice a bee on the sill, dead.

My son heads into the yard. I scoop the bee into my hand.

"Look at all these bugs!" he says. Once terrified of stinging insects, now he creeps up to a flower as slowly as he can to avoid spooking the bee crawling inside.

"I think it's him but I can't really see," he whispers loudly. Then, "We need bigger flowers!"

I am waiting for an opportunity to open my fist and discard the dead bee, but when he goes back into the house I find I cannot do it. Instead, I kneel and discreetly place the bee among the flowers, then cover him with soil.

The back door bangs open and he blasts out holding the horrendous cardboard bee house. He runs to our plum tree and hangs it from a low branch thick with pink blossoms and buzzing insects.

"We need to plant more plants, for their food," he says. "And bigger flowers."

I do not answer for some reason, but I will do that, I decide, right now, with my son. We will try to save the bees.

Into the Brainforest

The first time I tried to find an elementary school on the Key Peninsula, as an eager volunteer tutor, I was given directions that led me to a fish hatchery. It was an easy mistake. Schools and hatcheries are both common enough in our region and even resemble each other in the mildly nondescript manner common to most public institutions. Both are located near important streams, whether it's Minter Creek or the Key Pen Highway. Both share the design of interconnected structures in which the fry, whether fish or human, are moved to larger and larger pools of water or talent. And at a certain age each releases their charges into their respective societies to prosper and multiply, or to be consumed.

There are three elementary schools on our peninsula and I have volunteered at all of them. This is neither my fault nor a point of pride. Anyone who counts a teacher as a friend will understand that once you have set foot in a classroom, you are doomed. "Oh, you like pizza, come help my kids learn to cook this week." "Oh, your mother was an accountant, you should help teach my unit on math this month." "Oh, you know how to read, come help our students learn. All year."

What is worse, after having once stepped over the threshold, you want to do these things. But to be a successful classroom volunteer, it is essential that you preserve your integrity. This begins with punctuality: never arrive at school on time for anything. By arriving ten minutes after the morning bell, for example, you avoid the demolition derby of enraged parents ejecting reluctant students from speeding mini vans. More important, punctuality sends the wrong message. You get a reputation for responsibility, your life is over.

It is a lesson I fail to learn every year.

"Mr. Ted! Mr. Ted!" I am barely through signing in at the office when a young girl crushes me in a bear hug. She is a fourth grader I tutored the year before and who had once screamed "YOU'RE MEAN!" at me in front of her class after a dispute over contractions. Now she is glad to see me. I'd heard the family had lost their home on the Key Pen and that she was not to return, so I am glad to see her, too. I ask where she is living now.

"In a church!" she says, rolling her eyes.

A staff member leans over the office counter and slaps a VOLUNTEER sticker on my chest.

"Welcome back," she says.

I am sitting in a hallway with a third grade boy staring at a book written for children half his age. His gaze roams the hallway, seeking anything other than his task. I redirect him to the book on his lap. He points his head toward it without looking. "All we have to do is read this and you're done," I remind him. He looks down the hall.

I have been trained to be positive and encouraging while respectfully addressing the mistakes of struggling readers. But now I am tapping the first word of the title on the title page. "Anybody home?" I ask.

"THE" he blurts. I am tap-tap-tapping while remaining positive. "This is your only way out," I say.

He lurches forward and stumbles through the text, reading with laborious, halting, angry effort. I do not interrupt him to address his mistakes. There are too many. Instead, I say, "Keep going." It seems more important to finish the book than to get it right just now. He reads on. Words drop from his mouth like sour milk clop-clop-clopping from a carton. His eyes well up.

"It's just practice," I say. "It's all right."

Later, I am in the teacher's lounge stealing someone's cream for a cup of the coffee that has been warming in its carafe for most of the summer. A staff member eating lunch on her feet asks what I think of the boy from the hall. I say he needs more than my meager input. "There are obstacles," she says, looking at me in a way that makes me think I should understand.

She adds, "It's so important that he spend time with responsible adults." I nod, waiting for more. "Good, thank you," she says and walks away. I realize I have just signed up for a year in the hallway.

I go to the cavernous gym where children are sitting in

long rows at folding plastic picnic tables eating their lunches. I am looking over trays of fruit and rice and hot dogs when I see the boy from the hall at a crowded table. The only space left is on either side of him. He is drowning a hot dog in ketchup and mustard and perhaps some things less digestible. His classmates ignore him. I sit down.

"You want some hot dog with that?"

He slides the mess he's made over to me. "You eat it," he sneers.

I shove the dripping hot dog into my mouth. He stares.

"Awful," I say.

He looks at the table and asks, "I'm a good kid, aren't I?"

Part of Nature

I have blown up two lawn mowers since moving to the Key Peninsula, one while I was riding it.

The first incident occurred when I ran an electric push mower into a wall of blackberry vines. Rather than carefully backing it out, I gunned the throttle and the motor burst into flames.

I returned to the house with a new respect for blackberries, a difference I tried to convey to my wife. She listened in silence and then asked, "So what are you going to do about them?"

"I'm doing it," I said, and walked down to the bay with my fly rod.

The lawn had troubled me for some time. I had already destroyed it once out of frustration by spinning doughnuts across the surface in my neighbor's Suburban. I failed to make amends with several pounds of some kind of grassy fertilizer premix that stained the ground blue and smelled like burning plastic.

Then the moles came. They were the only living things in the large empty space surrounding our home. The ground was covered with dead or dying moss, scorched blackberry vines, and molehills. It was my understanding that moles lived on grubs and other subterranean insects that damaged young lawns, but there could be nothing here to sustain them.

My wife consulted a local militant gardener.

"I'm Talus," she said, looking down. She slipped out of her Birkenstocks and stroked the dying earth with the soles of her feet. She had the letter "P" tattooed on top of her left foot and "C" on the right, surrounded by lots of swirls and pointy things. I imagined these were meant to be some kind of totemic power symbols.

"You need clover," she pronounced. "Stat."

"Isn't that, like, a weed?" I asked.

"Lawns kill." She regarded me through blond dreadlocks. Then she chanted some ancient curse: "You poison nature to grow your grass, you plant clover to save your ass."

"Will that get rid of the moles?"

"They're part of nature," she said, which I took to mean no.

My wife invited Talus over to consult, a lot, and for some reason began paying her. She would appear in our yard without warning, wearing the same Birkenstocks and faded mechanic's coveralls with the sleeves rolled up to her tattooed elbows. She was unusually reticent on any subject other than growing things, but we knew she was part of an old Key Pen family and that she worked as an itinerant gardener up and down the peninsula. It was hard to tell her age. Her hands were lean and tough and always dirty. She kept her face shielded by the flapping coils of blond hair gone brown and matted. She came bearing sacks of seeds and instructions that she studiously repeated to my wife and our eight-year-old boy, but never to me. This, I felt, meant I was free to ignore her orders, and my boy and I instead ran around the yard pelting each other with handfuls of tiny gold pellets that would stick to our hair and clothes for weeks.

My wife took her vegetable garden more seriously. Talus responded with curious plants and exotic solutions. One day she strolled up our gravel drive leading a squadron of hungry ducks. They descended on the nascent garden with gusto, eating every slug within a half-mile radius. When Talus simply walked away down our drive, the ducks waddled noisily after her, leaving behind a generous deposit of fertilizer.

Then came William the Conqueror, a remarkably lazy and ugly goat whom Talus turned loose on our blackberry problem. He stood motionless for much of the time, idly chewing on a vine without enthusiasm, lost in thought. He did have the ingenuity to drift unseen into the garden one day. "It's goat soup tonight," I thought. But no. Instead of banishing him, or even tying him up, Talus immediately erected a fence around the garden by stretching nearly invisible fishing line between bamboo stakes about chest height, or eye level to the average quadruped. From these lines she suspended compact discs recorded by musicians who had died of overdoses long before CDs came into existence. Their discs spun forlornly in the slightest breeze, causing an irregular series of blinding flashes that irritated both the goat and me in equal measure, forcing both of us back to our assigned tasks.

Unlike William, however, who made slow progress deeper into the brambles, I did nothing for the yard. The boy and I had enjoyed our seed fights, and that seemed enough. Talus and I saw things differently, and rather than debate the merits of our conflicting worldviews regarding nature, I stayed out of her way.

I was not completely hostile to the notion of letting nature take its course in our lives. A few years before, a baleful woodpecker had taken over our roof as his personal one-bird drum circle, signaling his availability to any interested female within hearing by hammering his beak into our gutters, flashing or chimney at deafening velocity. He was one of the so-called Blackhearted Yellowhammers, or Northern Flicker, a notorious character in woodpecker lore, infamous for driving humans mad with merciless drumming on their structures. After months of this treatment, and after defeating multiple attempts to dislodge him, we had struck upon the idea of surrender. We nailed a two-foot tall woodpecker house to the apex of our roof, covering his favorite drumming spot. After some skeptical hesitation, the woodpecker took possession and prospered with a mate and a brood of young Yellowhammers.

That act of appeasement to nature was as far as I was prepared to go. I intended to call on professionals to deliver and install a lawn the moment Talus's work was completed and she was gone.

But things began to grow: mostly dandelions and moss. The moles, too, were reinvigorated and pushed up dirt

volcanoes all over the yard. I had already prepared myself
with a fine new riding mower in anticipation of lots of grass
to mow. Instead, I took to careening across this hardpan in
pursuit of the boy and his playmates, shouting "Banzai!" as
they hurled water balloons at my head. This seemed a fitting
use of the equipment until I hit a molehill at speed in the
midst of a turn and rolled the mower onto its side, spilling
fuel and oil which both immediately ignited. The children
responded with a barrage of water balloons.

My wife appeared with a fire extinguisher. Our boy was
delighted. "Look Mom! He did it again!"

"It's just part of nature," I said. My wife hit me with a
water balloon.

"I thought you were on fire," she said.

After we doused the flames, our teenaged neighbor
ambled into the yard. He was a skinny seventeen-year-old,
sporting all the gangly indifference of his species, yet still
irresistibly drawn to fire and destruction.

"Problem with your new mower?"

The machine lay smoldering on its side. The engine
cowling had melted along with one of the front tires, and
half the steering wheel was gone. After some negotiation,
we managed to right the machine and push it down the road
and into his yard amidst the carcasses of several cars he was
cannibalizing to build one that ran for more than a week.
He would do what he could with my mower, he said. I
handed him some cash and said, "Do more."

I walked back up the road. There was Talus, standing
on the edge of the freshly scorched circle of earth, pawing
the ashes with one of her decorated feet. Her head was

slightly bowed but she kept her eyes on me the way a herding dog tracks some stray steer before clamping onto its leg.

"You need help," she said.

"I just incinerated a two thousand dollar lawn mower. The only thing I need now is beer."

"What you need is goat blood, and lots of it," she said. "That, or bobcat urine. Desiccated, of course. That'll drive your moles insane. Then I can heal the soil. If you'll let me."

Putting any of those things in my soil seemed more likely to drive me insane, or at least attract the attention of curious bobcats and angry neighbors. "Since you mention it," I said, "I'm thinking more of a massive chemical fertilizer attack." I had not been thinking anything of the kind, but the way she aimed her head at me was starting to grate.

"And what about them?" she demanded, extending a tattooed arm toward the enormous woodpecker house on our roof. Three juvenile flickers jockeyed for position in the entrance hole, aiming their savage scimitar beaks down at us.

"Well, what about them?" I was not proud to have woodpeckers living on my roof. They were not the best of tenants, excavating our yard with enthusiasm and noisily debating woodpecker issues within their woodpecker house, but this accommodation had at least brought the endless drumming to an end.

"They eat insects, like your grubs and your ants. If you poison the insects, you'll poison the birds, and the animals that eat the birds, the hawks, the coyotes. And then there's the salmon. Do you want to poison the salmon, the eagles that eat them, the Orcas?"

"They're not my insects."

"Well, whose are they then?" She put her hands on her hips. The phrase hung in the air between us.

"Yeah," she said. "Think about it."

I took a step toward the house.

"Anyway. That's not why I'm here." Talus looked everywhere around her but not at me. "I need a ride."

She just stood there, hands still on her hips, taking in the scenery. Maybe accommodation would work on her the way it had with the woodpecker.

We drove south down the Key Pen highway toward the unfettered tip of the peninsula. The homes here were fewer and older, with large tracts of forest and farm dividing small neighborhoods or encircling reclusive families. I theorized that Talus's was one of these. Her ability to appear and disappear without warning was no longer mysterious: she had no car. She simply moved from one job to another hitching rides, often with sacks of seed or baskets of vegetables in her arms. I often saw her standing in Key Center, a local crossroads with a store, tavern and smoke shop, seemingly waiting for a ride, but never sticking her thumb out. I wondered who on the peninsula could tolerate her well enough to transport her and her livestock.

"What's that 'P' and 'C' on your feet stand for? 'Politically Correct?'"

"Pacific Crest," she said, staring straight ahead. "As in the trail from Canada to Mexico."

"Long walk."

"Turn here."

We passed through a curtain of dark woods onto a gravel road marked only by an old carved sign that read, "Vale." The road sloped steeply away from the highway, tunneling down into dark forest. The thick canopy above filtered the light to a hazy green. Long twisting branches cast a web of shadows over a floor of ferns that glowed in the peculiar twilight. The smell of damp earth and cedar bark flowed downhill with us until we emerged through a low opening in the tangle of trunks onto a small clearing. Talus had her head aimed in that angry herd dog way, as if ready to bash through the windshield at the slightest provocation. "It's Mother's place," she said.

There was an older model pickup truck with a cracked windshield haphazardly parked in front of an aging cabin. Patches of mismatched shingles decorated most of the building, while tarpaper covered one whole side. Under the tarpaper I could see the faint outline of a doorway high above the ground, leading into a room that either no longer existed, or that was waiting to be built. The cabin was awash in a giant's crazed jungle of enormous heirloom tomato plants and grape vines leaning into each other for support. The ground was thick with eruptions of root vegetables and the twisted ropes of shiny green melons, all surrounded by towers of corn and giant sunflowers standing guard like radiant sentinels in a child's fairy tale.

The porch at the front of the house was built from a collection of pilings and joists and other found material. Standing there was a large woman in a simple yellow floor length sundress. She looked to be about sixty or so, with a weathered face and a froth of hair bright with silver and yellow blond sprouting from her head like corn tassels. A tall, thin man in his late twenties, wearing ragged jeans and a sleeveless black tee shirt, stood there, too. He had been facing the woman but turned around when we pulled in. He was unshaven, except for his head. He folded his arms and stared at me.

Talus got out of the car. "You wait here," she said.

She walked straight toward the man without glancing in any other direction, climbed the porch and stood in front of him. The man continued staring at me.

I got out of the car and leaned against the hood, staring back. He was taller than Talus, taller than any of us, and he leaned over and into Talus when he spoke. He unfolded his arms and pointed a finger at her face. She slapped it away with a loud smack.

"Do you want to play with me?" A small voice sang from the garden. A little girl, about four or five, was sitting in a mud puddle tending a herd of tiny plastic animals. Her bright green eyes looked straight into mine. She wore the same kind of golden sun dress as the older woman and had long, bright blond hair generously decorated with fresh mud.

I kneeled down in front of her, keeping an eye on the porch. "What are we working on?"

"The animals are learning swimming," she said. She tipped water from a long-necked steel watering can into a hole she had dug.

"What are their names?"

"We just call them what they're called." She picked up a zebra. "This is Zebra. He's scared of swimming." She stood him up in the mud hole. "Don't be scared little zebra." She handed me a plastic pterodactyl. "He's Teriyaki."

I dipped Teriyaki in the mud hole, then stood him up next to it. "He can dry his wings in the sun."

"That's smart of him," she said.

"What's your name?"

"Clover."

I heard a car door squeak open behind me and the pickup truck came angrily to life. The man threw it into gear and lurched it backward, then spun around and tore off up the drive into the cedars, gravel popping like pistol shots under the wheels. Clover watched him go. "That's daddy."

"What are you doing?" asked Talus. "You're so muddy." She looked only at the girl but I could see her lips were trembling.

"Come play with us," said Clover.

"Gramma says you were totally clean like five minutes ago."

"I'm sorry, Mommy."

"Come on, let's get changed. I've got to get back to work."

"Can't we play first?"

"No."

"Um," I said. "How 'bout we just see you tomorrow, if you want?"

Talus nodded, then sank to her knees next to us. She jerked her chin toward the gravel drive. "That's the 'was-band.' Wants 'reimbursement,' you know, for sometimes being around." She nodded at her daughter.

I stood up. "Goodbye Clover."

"Goodbye." She waved Teriyaki at me.

The older woman, Gramma, was still on the porch. She smiled when I looked up, raised her arms and waved both hands at me, nodding.

I passed through the wall of tangled cedars and drove very slowly up through the tunnel of trees, embarrassed now by the sound of crunching gravel under my wheels. I emerged at the top of the road into the gray flat light and asphalt smell of the highway. I sat there for a few minutes for some reason, then drove north, toward home. But first I stopped at a local nursery and filled my hands with seeds for wild grasses, flowers, clover, and something called non-GMO Salmon Friendly Flowering Wheat Grass. I spent money for these lawn killers and, to ensure their growth, I ordered two dump trucks full of organic compost and topsoil.

The nurseryman at the register said, "Must be quite a project."

"I'm going to plant all this in my lawn," I said, patting a bag of seeds. "To protect the insects and birds and, you know, salmon, eagles."

"You're doing what now?" He closed his eyes as if my answer might blind him. I said I planned to plant these seeds all over my property and left it at that.

His hand hovered over the register. "I'm going to need some ID for your check."

A few days later, after my check cleared, I saw that two dump truck loads of organic compost and topsoil is a staggering volume of dirt. My plan was to spread these several tons over the whole yard of about an acre-and-a-half by wheelbarrow. After five wheelbarrow loads, I returned to the house for Advil and the phone book. Two hours later a small bulldozer was delivered by flatbed truck. Two minutes after that I was strapped in the cab and fiddling with joysticks trying to drive the thing. The machine made quick work of both spreading the dirt and tearing up the existing weeds and moss with its unforgiving treads, turning the soil and roots into long winding hummocks that resembled whale intestine.

Then came the seeding. I spent over a thousand dollars on the soil, seeds and bulldozer rental but wouldn't part with another ten bucks to buy a seed spreader. I was only going to use it once, I thought, so instead my son and I walked back and forth in a vaguely trapezoidal pattern throwing handfuls of seed onto the ground, into the air, and at each other in what was by then our standard practice.

Our teenaged neighbor slumped over to survey the project and get a turn driving the bulldozer. He inspected the mangled ground covered with haphazard arcs of seed and gray pellets of organic fertilizer that smelled faintly of death.

"Good luck mowing it," he said, then abruptly turned and walked home as if he'd forgotten something.

After some days of unexplained silence, Talus returned to us with undiminished passion. She weeded our garden, tended the fruit trees, and assaulted a sudden deer infestation with that withering bowed-head scowl of hers. She confronted the mole problem by pouring gallons of desiccated animal urine, castor oil, and worm casings into the tunnel system that surrounded our home. Nothing worked. She refused my offer to provide some bear-trap like devices designed for moles on the grounds that they were inhumane. Instead, she took to stabbing the earth with sharpened sticks and jamming burning road flares into the holes to drive the moles away with smoke.

This approach had no demonstrable effect on the moles, though we eagerly agreed with Talus that it must be bad for their morale. Attacking an invisible enemy with wands of burning magnesium also seemed to be good for her and that, to us, was worth something.

But Talus remained an enigma. She would spend long stretches walking up and down the length of our property, preparing plants for winter and periodically incinerating an emerging molehill. Her dreadlocks gave way to a wave of white blond hair she let float in the breeze, attracting leaves, insects and flower petals. She said nothing of Clover, of the 'was-band,' or her life outside our yard. When at last there was nothing more she could do for us, she disappeared.

We spent the long, wet winter that followed waiting to see what would emerge from our escapade. Strange leaves of grass appeared all around us as spring approached. Purple and yellow buds covered the lawn, mixed with patches of red and white clover. Tall strands of wildflowers grew out of nowhere, weighed down by enthusiastic bees. Our woodpeckers and robins and thrushes hopped madly in the grass, stalking whatever insects now dwelled within this wild prairie garden. Rabbits appeared. Then quail. Then a ring-necked pheasant. Of course, the deer returned in force. All were shadowed by our boy, crawling through the high grass with one of the sharpened sticks Talus had left behind.

Our slump-shouldered teenage neighbor came roaring up the road one day after successfully rebuilding my blown-up mower. He had replaced the melted steering wheel with one from a forgotten Volkswagen he found rusting in his yard, and he'd done something to the muffler to make it whine like a race car. When I climbed aboard, my wife followed with the fire extinguisher.

Our boy ran out in front of us, waving a spear.

"Stop! Don't mow the lawn down! We're part of nature now! We're part of nature!"

I turned the key, gunned the deafening engine, and drove the mower into the garage.

That Malevolent Society
of Peninsula Poets, Pedants,
and Provocateurs

The hitchhiker leaned into my passenger window, rain streaming off the brim of his soggy leather cowboy hat and onto his famously ancient, yellowing beard.

"There's an emergency meeting of the Society."

"Where?"

"Down at The 302," he said, twisting his head to stare at me with his good eye.

"Get in."

To most people, his statement would suggest heading south on the winding two-lane blacktop called State Route 302. But that road just flirts with the northern tip of the Key Peninsula for a few curvy miles, running past scattered homes and lonely espresso stands, before slicing west along curtains of trees toward Case Inlet and the Olympic mountains.

To the hitchhiker with the yellowing beard, it meant going to a bar.

He swung open the door and the truck heeled over as he settled himself onto the wet seat. He was a frequent and forlorn figure on our peninsula roadsides, often standing next to an aging motorcycle known for its avalanche-inducing engine noise and inability to run more than a few minutes at a time. Yellowbeard never bothered to stick a thumb out. The sight of him standing next to his machine, smoke rising from its carburetor or battery or brake pads, was enough to communicate a need for transport.

"You want to load up the bike?" I asked.

"Hell no. Nobody's gonna steal that damn thing."

Rainwater poured off his hat and onto his leather vest and jeans jacket, and big drops glistened in his long beard. The beard had once been black, then gray, and was on its way to white when a yellow halo appeared around his mouth, caused by the cigarettes so often found there. The discoloring radiated outward and down below his chin where it met another shade of yellow working its way in from the edges, a result of the many hours he spent in the sun picketing local establishments or standing on roadsides waiting for a lift.

The dashboard groaned against his knees and emitted an unsteady buzzing sound.

"You want to strap your seatbelt on?"

"No."

"Well, that buzzing you're hearing won't stop till you do."

Yellowbeard tilted his head to listen to the dashboard, then swiveled it the other way, squinting at me with his good eye. "If you say so, but I've been hearing that sound for fifty years at least."

I drove south on 302.

"Whoa, whoa, whoa," he said. "Bear right up here at the hog farm."

We approached a fork in the road and I slowed to make a soft right past a large field of lavender and hops. There were no hogs in sight, nor had there been for a generation.

Roads depicted on any decent map of the Key Pen resemble a grid slightly askew with dead ends that trail off in artsy curlicues. Once called the Indian Peninsula, the shape of the land vaguely resembles an old fashioned key, which led to a name change after a local contest held for that purpose in the 1930s. But on the ground the peninsula is a hypnotic maze of randomly named dirt and gravel lanes spiraling off the highway through tunnels of trees no sane person would enter uninvited. Like so many longtime locals, Yellowbeard found it easier to navigate this terrain by referring to landmarks long ruined, or that no longer existed.

The 302 tavern itself, in a sense, had ceased to exist when the original establishment burned down in 1969. It was called "Lou's Place," after the owner, but the locals of that era had called it The 302 because it sat on the shoulders of that highway and was easy to find back then. Locals would tell their off-peninsula friends, "You just cross the bridge and drive down 302 and when you get to a bar, stop."

Lou Serka, part of a venerable Croation family of loggers and fisherman, relocated and reestablished the tavern twice under two subsequent names, including the current "Sven's Grill and Grotto," winding up far and away beyond the reaches of State Route 302. But his place is still called The 302.

"Here, pull in at the mill," said Yellowbeard, pointing to the gated entrance of a local winery. The rusty boiler and stack of a small steam-powered lumber mill, defunct since World War II, were just visible on the edge of the vineyard.

"What are we doing here?"

"Gettin' some wine!" He climbed out of the truck and the springs sighed as they expanded to their normal height. He shrugged his way through a sheet of rain to the closed tasting room, hammered on the door, then returned moments later with a bottle of white wine stuffed in his jacket.

"Why are you bringing wine to a bar?"

"What?" Yellowbeard struggled to buckle himself back in, but only succeeded in wrapping the shoulder strap around his arm. "What kind of crazy Houdini crap is this?"

The 302, Sven's Grill and Grotto, is on a narrow road popular with scenery-seeking drivers and a short walk uphill from a marina busy with voyagers in summer. The building had served as a small barn since shortly before the turn of the last century and collapsed in on itself sometime before the turn of this one. Lou Serka bought it to salvage the timber, it was assumed, but instead he cut out the rotted remains of the lower walls, leaving just the loft, and moved his bar into it. The result was a squat barn that appeared to be sinking into the soggy roadside with eaves nearly touching the ground.

I pulled up to the front door and stopped. Yellowbeard unwound himself from the seatbelt while clutching the bottle in his jacket. "Why don't you join us today? Remember, it's an emergency."

"What is?"

"We're gonna impeach the whole county council!"

It was a long room with a low, bare plank ceiling and the heavy scent of wood smoke, tobacco, and damp, moldering decay. Mounds of dust clung like moss to rafters crudely milled from old growth timber. The head of a snarling black bear was mounted over the bar. Around its neck dangled a sign that read, "Dissatisfied Customer." Beneath this were half a dozen beer taps embellished with handwritten labels that read either "foreign" or "domestic." The domestic label seemed to indicate beer made in Washington and named after some part of it, like Rainier or Olympia. Foreign meant it came from Seattle.

There was a ratty cougar skin nailed to the wall opposite the bar, together with wagon wheels, a long, two-handed saw with jagged, rusting teeth, a logger's spring-board, and about three dozen sets of confiscated car keys. Under this was a rectangular wood stove next to a long wooden table covered with beer glasses, coffee mugs, newspapers, and yellow legal pads. Along the wall was a heavy bookcase holding a fat dictionary, miscellaneous encyclopedias, almanacs, and old magazines. One of these had a picture of the Berlin Wall on the cover with the headline, *What if it Fell?*

Yellowbeard sat down at the table among a few other longtime locals whom I knew to be his confederates in a loose association of community anti-activists devoted to preserving the Key Peninsula by opposing any change to it in any form. They had been meeting for years, I understood, at first to discuss books they read, poetry they wrote, and politics they opposed. But the group had quickly devolved into a coven of gadflies so obstreperous they'd been banished from the meeting rooms of our local library and community center. They could not even agree what to call themselves, rejecting several variations of "The Society For," "The Society Against," and "The Society of," and had come to be known by outsiders simply as *that* Society.

A small man at one end of the table glared at me. He was about seventy, wearing a brown plaid blazer with a wide yellow tie and a jaunty, forest green snap-brim hat like those worn by Alpine trekkers, at least in the movies. It was pulled low over his forehead, the angle of the brim matching that of his nose so that in profile he resembled an irritated finch. He pointed a pen at me.

"Is that yours?" he asked Yellowbeard.

"What?" Yellowbeard pulled the wine bottle out of his jacket and put it on the table in front of another man. He was much older, had white hair sprouting from the sides of his head and wore a heavy flannel shirt. He was bent over a legal pad.

"That's for the chowder, Lou," said Yellowbeard. "Get your boy to open that."

Lou squinted at the bottle. "Oh yes, I see it's the good stuff. Hey, Rusty?" Lou raised his head up to look toward the bar.

"This is a private meeting," said Finch.

"Get on with it," said the one woman at the table. She was tall and lanky, looked to be in her fifties or sixties and had a bundle of fading red hair stuffed into a brightly colored knit cap. She knocked a heavy cane against the table as she spoke, then held a hand out and smiled, revealing a space where her left canine tooth had been. "I'm Big Junior."

Finch continued: "We're here to swear out arrest warrants for members of the county council due to their dereliction of duty concerning our demand for the instant removal of Western Cedar Beach Road in the vicinity of Indian Rock Creek, failure to do so being just cause for the Key Peninsula to secede from said county."

"And do what?" asked Big Junior.

"Join Mason County."

"What? That's across the water," said Lou.

"I don't like the cops over there," said Yellowbeard.

"Or anywhere," said Big Junior, winking at me.

"We can form our own county since we're essentially an island, physically and philosophically," said Finch. "I'd suggest Key Island County."

All of us looked at him. "We just have to cut some bridges," he added.

"Now that's a good idea," said Yellowbeard, slapping the table.

"What? It's a terrible idea," said Big Junior. "These are terrible, terrible ideas. Cutting bridges? A new county? What exactly is it you're drinking anyway?" She banged her cane for emphasis.

"Nothing yet," said Yellowbeard, picking up the wine bottle. "Where's Rusty? Rusty!"

A large man with a gray ponytail and goatee came out from behind the bar. He grabbed the bottle of wine by the neck. "Are you kidding me with this?"

"Oh, there you are," said Lou, "Open that for us, will you, and bring out the chowder."

Rusty looked at Yellowbeard. "You know we sell wine here."

"What?"

Rusty stared at him. I picked up the magazine with the Berlin Wall on the cover. "You've got quite a collection here. It's like a museum."

"It is a museum. That's one of our problems." He walked away holding the wine bottle like a club.

"Why do we want the road removed?" asked Big Junior. "That was never part of the plan."

Lou answered. "They want to put in a bridge down there. Another bridge!"

"It's an obvious attack on our sovereignty," said Finch. "A waste of tax dollars. And a clear zoning violation."

"We have to hit back," said Yellowbeard. "They build a bridge, we take it out!"

"The county wants to control us," said Lou.

"The county wants to maintain the roads," said Rusty, "which we need for driving on." He put the now open bottle of wine on the table together with a few tumblers. "They want to install a culvert to let salmon through and pave it so people will visit. Thirsty people."

"It's your classic land grab," said Lou, waving Rusty away.

"How's that?" I asked.

"The salmon don't need help from the government," said Finch. "That's just a smokescreen."

Rusty returned with a tray bearing small bowls of white broth that smelled of butter and garlic and seawater. "Finally," said Lou. He held a bowl under his chin and began spooning chowder into his mouth. "We put some of our own geoduck in this."

"The government is after our shellfish, too," said Finch, appraising the bowls but making no move toward them. "They want to regulate it out of our hands and send it straight to Japan."

"Regulations!" said Lou. "What can you do?"

"Stop them building another bridge," said Finch. "How else can we defend ourselves?"

"They need a good road for their military vehicles, their troop carriers, is what it is," said Yellowbeard.

"And then there's the gangs," said Lou. "It's gonna be tanks or gangs when the spit hits the fan. People don't care what's at stake." Chowder ran down his chin as he spoke.

"We'd be saving the peninsula from itself," said Finch.

"About that," I said, "what's the problem with the salmon?"

"Salmon!" said Lou. "It's not about the salmon!"

"You must be unaware that our salmon spend years swimming as far away as Siberia," said Finch, addressing me. "Then they navigate back here to the streams where they hatched. They evade killer whales and sea lions and swim up rivers and leap over waterfalls with bears grabbing at them and eagles diving on them until they reach their home stream. Do you seriously believe a fish like that needs help crossing a road?" He snickered at my naiveté.

"Salmon cross roads?" I asked.

"Easily," said Finch.

"Haven't you ever seen it?" asked Big Junior.

"No."

"Well, there's your problem," said Yellowbeard. "Let's drink up and go." He refilled a tumbler.

"He can go alone, now," said Finch. "We need these warrants finished and notarized today."

"Well, I guess it is a little early to leave the bar," said Yellowbeard.

I felt a single heavy tap on my shoulder. Big Junior rested the handle of her cane there. "Let's take a ride," she said.

* * *

She drove slowly through the rain in her sky blue 1970-something pickup. We were on a wide gravel road I'd never seen before, somewhere south of The 302. She turned down a second unmarked road that followed a stream on one side, then sloped down to parallel the shore on the other.

Big Junior stopped the truck. There was muddy shoreline on our left with piles of driftwood and eelgrass. On our right was a barbed wire fence protecting a sodden field that rose gradually to a line of bare alder trees. Rain pounded on the steel roof and poured across the roadway, which is why I thought she stopped.

"You know any men?" she asked. "Good men, available men?"

"Um, let me think."

"It's an easy question."

"Well, come to think of it, no."

She kept looking out the windshield into the rain. "Why doesn't anyone ever answer 'yes' to that question?"

A cloud of crows swept over us from the water and past the trees on the far side of the field. I saw the large silhouette of an eagle perched on a high branch. Squadrons of crows split off from the main body and plunged toward the eagle, swept past, and reformed their cloud. The eagle didn't move.

"Those men back there," she said. "They're not good role models."

"I don't know," I said. "They make good malcontents."

"They're broken. They're not good for anything anymore, if they ever were. You shouldn't be there. You should be coaching soccer, or stuffing envelopes for the PTA. You don't belong in our Society."

I watched raindrops splash in the sheen of water flowing over the road. A two-foot long salmon leapt up from behind a piece of driftwood, landed on the pavement and shot across the road.

"Did you see that?" asked Big Junior.

"I don't know if I did or not."

Another fish emerged from the eelgrass, paused on the shoulder, then sent up an arc of spray as it wriggled through the quarter inch of water on the roadway and into the field, where it flopped over.

I got out of the truck and walked up the shoulder. Water pouring off the field nearly flowed over my boots. I could hear the crashing of the stream hidden beyond the line of alders and saw large puddles seeping out from it into the field. I approached the gasping salmon but kept my distance. It looked to be a foot and a half or two feet long, red and green striations barely visible under peeling gray skin. Its gills heaved and its ragged jaw gaped open and closed. The once fat, seagoing body had consumed itself to complete the return, leaving this gaunt, ruined blade of a creature. It flung itself upward, splashed in the grass and struggled forward for another foot or two before flopping over again. I could see the spray and splashing of more salmon swimming across the field, climbing toward the banks of the overflowing stream, and many more that were dead.

Fish kept shooting across the pavement, pulsing, slithering, their rotten hides coming off like snakes shedding their skins. Months earlier, somewhere in the ocean, a feeling welling up inside them said "NOW" and they turned back here, never resting, never eating, just swimming a thousand miles through a universe of signs we can barely grasp to reach their home waters and spawn before they died.

Big Junior came up behind me. "Watch this."

She took a few steps into the field, water covering her boots, and poked at a dead salmon with her cane. When it didn't move, she kneeled down and slipped the tip of her cane into its mouth and down its gullet. She stood up and held the cane over her head with both hands. The eagle in the alders dropped off its branch and glided toward us like it was on a wire. It reared back and flared its wings with a loud thud of air, spraying us with rainwater from its feathers. It swung out its enormous talons and grabbed the fish, then beat its wings and climbed away like a swimmer surfacing for air.

"We need a bridge," I said.

* * *

Eight months later, on a clear summer day, Big Junior and I stood again on the edge of the field. A handful of county officials sat on a row of folding chairs behind a podium placed on top of the new culvert. The culvert was at least eight feet in diameter but half of that was below sea level, and the newly paved road gently rose up and over it. The county had elected to put a guardrail along this small bridge, but the barbed wire fence was gone and the field had been excavated to funnel floodwater toward the culvert and into the saltwater of Puget Sound.

Finch skulked along the edge of the field, wearing his same brown plaid blazer, yellow tie and Alpine trekking hat. He stared into the culvert, then at the guardrail and its supports, as if marking them for demolition when sabotage would at last became necessary to save the peninsula from itself.

The officials took turns speaking into a microphone before a small crowd. They mentioned the benefits of new public land, local cooperation, and habitat restoration. Yellowbeard paced back and forth in front of them, wearing a sandwich board with the words "IMPEACH THE COUNT" on the front and the letter "Y" on the back. He wore his same leather cowboy hat and jeans jacket in spite of the heat. His face was red and damp. I caught his eye and waved him over.

"What is it, traitor?" he said, fixing his gray, blind eye on me.

"You don't look good. Why don't you shed a layer and sit down?"

"Nah. Rusty's got a spread for us waiting. I could use a lift." He swiveled his head around to look at me with his good eye.

"He ruined that place," said Big Junior. "I'm never going back there." Lou had passed away in the spring and Rusty wasted no time transforming Sven's Grill and Grotto into The Rusty Saloon. The relics that had once adorned it were replaced with big screen TVs, a pool table, and a new clientele.

"You must be very proud of your new bridge," said Finch from behind us.

"All I did was write a letter," I said.

"Using our data," he snapped.

"You don't have data. You have delusions."

"When the spit hits the fan, you'll wish you were on our side."

A representative from the local tribe stood before the microphone. She was a young woman in a long, tawny dress the color of her broad face, and she had black hair braided down the length of her back. While installing the culvert, the builders had uncovered a granite boulder with Native symbols carved into it. The boulder was only about two feet in diameter and had been found facing the water, buried below the high tide line by sediment. Now it sat on a wooden pallet near the podium with the carving facing the crowd. The figure was the size of a large hand span, and seemed to depict a human form surrounded by an elongated fish or abstract lines that might have been wings, or waves, or wind.

The representative held an abalone shell as she spoke. In it were some smoldering herbs and tobacco, which she idly fanned with large eagle feathers in her other hand.

"We will protect the stone in our museum. But before we remove him I invoke and remind us of his purpose here, and our purpose, too."

She drew the eagle feathers across the abalone shell once or twice and a large pillow of smoke emerged and dissipated around her and the officials nearby.

"Water follows water, flowing over and through every obstacle, bringing life and taking life. The stone that stood here for so long invited the salmon that sustained us to return to our waters. Its presence guided them home, as its presence guides us to honor what remains."

She moved the feathers rapidly across the shell, pushing smoke out over the stone and into the crowd.

Yellowbeard inhaled deeply. "I think that's my brand."

The last speaker was our county council member. He thanked the tribe, the construction company that built the road, and the residents of the Key Peninsula for supporting him. To prove his sincerity, he said, he brought with him the mascot of the Key Pen. He held up a giant clam by its meaty neck before the politely clapping crowd.

"Do you see that?" sputtered Yellowbeard.

"It's a geoduck," I said.

"It's an insult," said Finch. "It's a challenge. We are going to fight them on that."

"On what?" I asked.

"He's thrown down the gauntlet," said Finch. "This display of power on this bridge we fought against is the county saying it can do whatever it wants with us and our resources. Haven't you learned anything?"

"The fight is on!" said Yellowbeard.

"On what?" I repeated.

Yellowbeard swiveled his head toward me. "What?"

I reached up and put a hand on his shoulder to steer him toward my truck. "You need to get out of the sun. Let's get a drink."

We walked down the shoulder to where I had parked. I lifted the sandwich board off his shoulders and tossed it into the bed of the pickup. I turned the truck around since the new bridge was blocked by the ceremony marking its opening.

"Take that left down here past the water," said Yellowbeard. He pointed to a dark gravel lane through the woods at the end of the shoreline.

"That's the opposite direction of The 302."

"Yeah, but it ends up being faster."

At the edge of the water, I turned down yet another road I'd never seen before and headed into the trees. Water nearly surrounds the Key Peninsula. It's almost an island. You'd think it impossible to get lost in a place like that, on a thin strip of land. Most people don't. But there's a difference between that and finding what you're looking for.

The Saltwater We Know

I called to ask permission to borrow my kayak, but still felt like a thief when I took it off the rack in our garage.

"Whatever," my wife had said on the phone.

I strapped the kayak to the top of my truck. When I went back into the garage for the rest of my gear, the emptiness on the wall rack stood out. Two boats were left. All should be gone, or at least two. We never went paddling without our son in the short wooden kayak the three of us built together. He might notice that empty space when he came home from school. Perhaps I could get back and replace my kayak before then. It upset him to have me there and then leave. It upset all of us, for different reasons.

I put in at Wauna, a long rocky sandspit at the top of the peninsula, and paddled south toward a public park a few miles away. I was exhausted, but it was a bright, still day and I felt better the moment I was afloat. I couldn't remember the last time I'd been on the water alone. Not since our son could hold a paddle. He had been so eager but cried at first when he found how different it was to be alone in his own boat.

"Have you been drinking?" my wife asked when I

called about the kayak. I understood it was just a question. I was in a hospital sometime after sunrise. Borrowing the kayak came up as an excuse. The night before I'd been holding my mother's hands in the emergency room to keep her from ripping out an IV. They strapped her down to a gurney after she bit me. A paramedic leaned on her shins with gloved hands. A doctor and nurse experimented for an hour trying to sedate her. Her screams of, "Daddy, help me please, Daddy!" ceased only after the third drug. She continued to flinch and murmur, a sleeper trapped in a nightmare.

"It is so often this way with the elderly," said the doctor, "if they are compromised and, of course, if there is a history of dementia."

I'd seen it before. When they rolled her in from the ambulance, I handed the nurse a list of the fourteen different pills we made my mother swallow every day.

"Well, look at you," the nurse said without looking at me.

My mother was not having a stroke, or a seizure, or hemorrhage, or anything exotic. It was going to be something ordinary and preventable, like an infection or food poisoning from the facility where I had moved her from my home. Very little was required to collapse her ruined universe.

The nurse and the paramedic talked to each other. The paramedic said she was training for a triathlon. The nurse said he was into mud runs. The doctor was older, closer to my age, with a West African name. When we were alone, he said, "Tell me how you came to injure yourself."

He dabbed the side of my head with gauze that came away bloody. There was a small gash above my ear. I said something about living in a hotel room and banging my head on a nightstand when the call about my mom woke me. He scraped dried blood out of my hair and cleaned the injury. I described the call, the facility aide saying my mom was acting up and they'd called an ambulance. I did not say I had no memory of hurting myself.

"It is a terrible thing to see a parent this way. I have ordered antibiotics, which may calm her in the event she is simply reacting to infection. There is risk in this, too, as you are aware. With your permission, I will admit her."

His formality and attention were an unfamiliar comfort. I felt more blood running down the side of my face, but it was a tear. The doctor moved my mom into a room at dawn. I sat there in the dark waiting for daylight before calling home.

"No, I haven't been drinking," I said. I understood it was just a question.

The shore near Wauna is crowded with small houses. You get the feeling you're paddling through someone's yard. No one waves back when you float by. The land gradually rises into steep, unpopulated bluffs that drop down to the water's edge. I missed the quiet of floating on saltwater, the shifting green and blue in the sunlight that makes the colors ashore dull and uniform. Even on flat water there is a subtle rolling expansion of the surface that is felt more than seen, like breath filling a body. It can carry you away if you let it.

If I was going to get the kayak back before my son came home from school, I would have to turn around soon.

Instead of paddling all the way to the park, I aimed for a thin strip of rocky beach that is open to the public only below the high tide line of driftwood and seaweed.

I carried the kayak over the rocks to avoid scratching the wood hull. I stretched and drank water. Usually I brought beer. That would've been a mistake today, maybe, I thought. Then I wondered how big a mistake.

"Hello," said a small voice.

A little girl about five- or six-years-old appeared on the beach in front of me. She wore a faded sundress and muddy sandals, and smiled at me with a big grin that was missing two or three front teeth.

"Hello," I said. "I didn't see you there. Your dress kind of blends in with the beach."

"What are you doing?" she asked.

"Taking a break. What are you doing?"

"I'm painting the sky." She raised both hands and looked toward the sun, wiggling her fingers. "You know that blue you get the way flowers look like in the morning that's not really dark blue but it's like it's this strong blue? It's that color. Do you like that color?" She pointed to the sky.

"That is a strong blue."

"I think more. It's better with paints but I ran out. They give me them at school."

She moved her hands and fingers like leaves drifting on a breeze. The beach felt warm. The sun cast our shadows across the embankment behind us, but more shadows moved among them as pools of sunlight formed and shifted and broke apart on the water.

"Why aren't you in school now?"

"Daddy took me out when he got mad at them. You know my Daddy."

She looked familiar but I couldn't place her. My son was close to her age but older. Her eyelids were swollen and her cheeks smeared with something like dirt and maybe that blue she was describing.

"Have you been crying?"

"Yes."

"Why?"

"I'm actually lost."

I looked around the beach. There was no one on the shoreline and no sound but the lapping of water on the rocks.

"You're here alone?"

"Yes."

"Well, you found me. What's your name?"

"Clover. You know. From Gramma's, remember?"

The sound of her name brought her back to me the way a familiar scent summons a feeling. She was the daughter of a gardener my wife had hired almost a year before. I had met Clover only once at her grandmother's, in the summer. Her parents were both there, already divorced but still fighting. My own family was intact then. Nothing had happened yet to cleave our life into the lives we lived now. That's why I had lost my memory of her, I thought. Clover was from that other life.

"Where's your mom?"

"I guess working. Daddy's at the road. I'm not to cross it. Should you take me back there?"

I moved the kayak high up on the beach and followed Clover as she walked further south, under the bluffs. I tried to pull my phone from a pocket and discovered I was still wearing my life jacket. There was no indication that a call would reach anyone, and I wondered who to call in any case. Clover strode down the beach, then abruptly turned and climbed a narrow cut in the sandy embankment. We pulled ourselves up by the roots of trees piercing the bluff until we were under a blanket of tottering madrona and twisting cedar and spruce with drooping branches pointing in all directions. Clover ducked and wove her way under and through a narrow path of ferns and brush but it seemed a very long one for a six-year-old to have traveled alone.

We came to a muddy pasture bounded by four strands of gray wire that I thought must be electrified. Clover slipped between them without slowing.

"Where are you going?"

"This way. Careful or it's going to sting you," she said.

I crawled between the two lower lines and trotted to catch up. A couple of large animals stood further up the slope in the direction Clover was headed. They turned their heads toward us and began to run.

"Clover, wait."

"It's okay."

They were big, dark colored llamas. They ignored Clover but came within a few yards of me, aggressively swiveling their heads back and forth, examining me with each eye and then head on. They flared their nostrils and snorted disapproval. I followed Clover and they followed me at an interested distance, spitting at my heels.

She walked along a watercourse that ran through the pasture, then slipped through another set of wires and continued along a creek overhung by spindly vines with a few delicate, solitary flowers. I could not remember the last time I'd hiked cross-country, headlong, blind, a trespasser. I didn't know where I was or how I would get back. I would not make it home in time to return the kayak before my family returned. I had to call my wife to warn her. I had to call the hospital to check on my mom. I would have to drive her back to her facility that night. And then I would have to meet her in ER again someday, soon.

Clover stopped and held up a small flower from a dangling vine.

"This is that blue I like," she said. She didn't pluck the flower, just held it up. Her fingers were stained with paint.

The stream ran through a culvert under a road that stopped our progress. We climbed the embankment of ivy and thorns and emerged onto the two-lane road and kept walking. Vehicles passed, slowing and then speeding away. They were looking at a little girl in a sundress followed by an unwashed older man in muddy rubber boots and a life jacket.

We came to a small tavern called The 302, a sway-backed old wooden building that had once been a barn. It was stained nearly black by time except for the bright moss on its roof. I knew it well.

"Daddy's in there," said Clover. "But he says I can't come in."

I held out my hand. Clover grabbed on to me without hesitation, the same way she had climbed the bluff, slipped through the fence, marched past the llamas. I pulled the door open and we stepped into the warm smell of alcohol and tobacco. There were men mostly, faces lit by beer signs behind the bar. A woman on a stool by the door swiveled around with a drink in her hand. "She can't be here!"

I took a step forward to catch the bartender's eye. She was a young woman, out of place by a decade at least, staring at me with big eyes. I saw no one I recognized.

"We're looking for this girl's father," I said.

"Don't look at me! I'm innocent this time!" said a loud man at the bar. The other men laughed and banged their glasses.

"You can't bring her in here!" the woman on the stool said again, slowly this time, so I could understand. The bartender disappeared into the kitchen.

"This little girl is lost. She says her father is in here."

The swinging door to the kitchen banged open and a figure came toward us. He was tall and narrow with a shaved head and stained tee shirt. I recognized her father but I stepped in front of Clover anyway. He moved around me without a glance and grabbed her hand out of mine. "I'm gonna beat your butt!" he said, pulling her outside.

"Can I watch?" said the loud man at the bar. There was more laughter and the men thumped their glasses on the bar again.

Outside, I said, "She was down on the beach."

Her father looked at me like I had called him a name. "Fine. Got it. Goodbye."

I pulled my phone out. There was no service but I dialed. "I'm calling 9-1-1 to report an endangered child," I said.

"Seriously? Seriously?" He threw his hands up in disgust. "She's supposed to wait in the truck! I told you stay in the truck! You got your books! You got your goddamn paints!" He leaned down over her, putting his hands on his knees. Her face turned red but there was no expression on it.

"Your truck?" I asked. "For how long?"

He looked up at me. "I'm working kitchen," he said, barely moving his mouth. He was a young man, not thirty. The bones stood out in his arms and shoulders. His eyes bulged in their sockets but they were clear. He smelled of disinfectant.

The door to The 302 slowly opened and a large, portly man with a gray beard and ponytail stepped out.

"What the hell is this?" he asked.

"How you doin', Rusty?" I extended my hand.

He looked at me for a long minute, then gave my hand a limp squeeze. "Where you been at? Haven't seen you in a while."

"I'm on a diet."

"You want your car keys back?"

"No, I like knowing where they are."

Clover's father stood up straight when Rusty appeared. He pointed at me with a stiff arm, like he was holding a gun. "Guy's callin' the cops."

"Why? You hurt his feelings?"

"I found his daughter down at the water, alone."

"I actually found you," said Clover.

"You shut up," said her father. "I mean, just hush up. You're supposed to wait in the truck."

Rusty appeared unmoved, but he said, "What's wrong with you? Just bring her into the office till you're done. Which will be soon." He glanced at me without saying anything else and went back into his bar.

Clover's father stared down at me from his full height. He smiled, showing off a few ragged teeth. "I know who you are, by the way. I remember you. You and my ex were, like, special friends, huh?"

"My wife hired her to work in our garden."

He nodded without changing his smile. "You're way too old for her, you know that, don't you? You're like, what, forty, fifty? You're older than her father was when he croaked."

"You know all about fatherhood."

"I know you can't tell me what to do."

I held up my phone. "Yes, I can."

He jerked forward but stopped himself. "Whatever." He turned back to the bar and pulled the door open. "Move it," he said. Clover followed him with that same blank expression. She held a hand up to me with paint stained fingers. The door closed and the warm smells of the place rushed past.

I walked back down the road to the culvert, looking at my phone with every step. No service, no service, no service. I slid down the embankment, followed the stream to the llamas' pasture, and slipped through the wires. The llamas ignored me. I walked under the trees, through the tangle of branches and ferns, and climbed down the bluff. The sun had passed over to the far side of the peninsula and the beach was in shadow and cold. My kayak was there, alone among the driftwood. The water had taken on the color of the sky, and that was a dark, strong blue.

King Tide

Rocky Creek begins life as a tiny spring trickling down a ravine about half a mile behind our place. The land around us slopes toward it slightly, but we notice that only in winter when it rains powerfully for days without stopping. After these stretches the ground is so saturated the rainfall moves in a body across our yard, through the woods and brush, over the edge of the ravine, and into the swelling creek. When I still lived there with my family, my wife and I would open the bedroom windows at night in spite of the cold and lay there listening to the water moving past us and crashing down the creek's course. We heard it tear trees from its banks and roll stones down to saltwater and into the wide bay the water had carved over time.

There is a simple, concrete boat ramp just west of that bay where the Key Peninsula begins its separation from the mainland. It's more of a gap in the guardrail on 302 above a slice of public beach, but it's ideal for a flat bottom boat at high tide when the water reaches the parking lot. I'd scouted it thoroughly by kayak, enough to know what tide height meant to water depth along that stretch of shore. There was a small window of only an hour or so to launch even a flat boat that drew more than a foot.

I remembered this when I lined up my trailer to back my new boat down the ramp and saw it blocked by a pickup truck with a large plastic crate in its bed. There was a long, low-sided aluminum skiff beached at the foot of the ramp filled with the largest salmon I had ever seen. The fish looked like a collapsed pile of cordwood too long to fit into anyone's stove.

Two Indians in vinyl bibs used both hands to fling the fish into the crate. They'd grab a salmon by the gills on each side of its head and swing it up tail first over the tailgate. The crate was nearly full, and so was their boat.

I walked up to what I thought was a respectful distance near the younger of the two men. He was tall, heavy, his black hair pulled tight behind his head, gloves and bibs smeared with blood. "How long you guys been at this?"

"All night, Mac, we go all night." It was the older man who spoke. He laughed without looking at me. He was about my height, but rounder, stronger, with a rusty face and gray halo around the edges of his wrinkled forehead that bled back into a loose pile of thinning hair.

"How much longer you gonna be?"

"Got a lot of fish here, Mac, a lot of Kings."

"Looks like it. Looks like you don't have enough room in your crate for 'em either."

"Nope, we do not, we do not at that," said the older man. He stopped what he was doing and looked at me. "You play any tennis?"

"What? No. Why?"

"Harold, look at this guy." He spoke to the younger man, who stopped tossing fish, stretched, and noticed me for the first time.

"You know who this is, right?" said the older man. Harold looked into my eyes and tugged at his gloves. He had a broad face with high cheekbones and a burnt red color, darker than the older man's.

"Should I?"

"It's friggin' John McEnroe, Harold, where you been?" The older man laughed and clapped and pointed.

"I don't know who that is," said Harold, who kept looking at me.

"He's a friggin' tennis star, man, look at him! Hey, Mac, can I have your autograph?"

"I don't play tennis," I said.

"Well you sure as all hell fooled me, Mac, because you sure as hell look like McEnroe," said the older man. "Whatever happened to him?"

"I don't know. I don't play tennis."

"Well you should. You look like you'd be good at it." He stood there looking at me.

I glanced at the pile of fish. "I need to get my boat in the water in an hour or I can't launch it. How about I give you a hand?"

"How about you go somewhere else."

"Because by the time I get somewhere else, the tide will be too low for me to launch."

He picked up a fish and lightly tossed it into the crate. "Suit yourself, Mac."

I climbed up the trailer to my boat and reached down into a locker for a pair of gloves used for hauling anchor line. I pulled them on and walked down to the Indian boat wondering when I'd last handled a whole fish. But that hardly mattered.

I grabbed the gills of a salmon and lifted. It slipped out of my grip and back into the pile. The Indians said nothing. There was a thick coat of slime covering the fish that made their dark silver skin shimmer and smell, but only faintly.

The next time I hooked my fingers into the gills and lifted straight up. The fish was about three feet long and heavier than it looked. I tried to swing it over the edge of the crate. It flopped onto the tailgate, opening a gash on its side.

"Easy, Mac, that's a nice King you got there, man, King Salmon. Don't go making him mad," said the older man. Then his phone rang. He pulled off a glove and dug in his pocket, pulled out a phone and flipped it open. "Yeah, Benny, where are you?"

"Uh, is this Bishop?" asked the caller.

"Yeah, it's Bishop, what the hell you think? Where are you? Wait, don't answer. Where's your boat that's supposed to be here?"

"Yeah," said the caller. "Didn't you talk to Roberta?"

"What the hell?" said Bishop. "I've got that friggin' Roberta's boat here, man. It's a joke. It's an embarrassment. I've got a friggin' white guy staring at it right now and he is simply appalled." Bishop winked at me. "You, Benny, you need to show up with your boat and do your job, now. We've got three more nets to pick and two days to do it."

Bishop flipped the phone closed and held it up to Harold. "You believe this guy?"

"What'd you expect?" asked Harold without stopping his work.

"I expect people to show up and do their jobs. I do, you do, he does," said Bishop, pointing the phone at me. "You do work, don't you Mac?"

"For the most part I just hang around Wimbledon and sell autographs."

Bishop waved the phone at me. "You see, Harold? He knows tennis. You should learn."

Harold said nothing.

We loaded fish into the crate and then filled the truck bed. My gloves, clothes and skin were covered with their slime, scales and blood.

We spoke little, mostly because Bishop took so many phone calls, alternately yelling at or cajoling disembodied voices to get him a decent-sized boat. He did allow that when he wasn't picking nets he was a large animal vet just up the road in Victor. Harold was a firefighter in Puyallup. Sometimes people walking the beach would ask to buy a fish, but all Bishop would say is they belong to the tribe and ignore them as he had tried to ignore me. At the end of an hour, the water had receded a good fifty yards, revealing a flat terrain of slick green seaweed and muddy shelves peppered with rocks.

When the fish were loaded, Bishop and Harold both pulled off their gloves and Bishop lit a cigarette. "So, Mac, where you going anyway?"

"It's too late to launch now," I said.

"Like hell. Back your trailer down here. Harold, get this thing out of the way." Bishop slapped the pickup. "And bring down that pry bar."

I watched Bishop in my rearview mirror as he impatiently rolled his hand back over and over, drawing me further out onto the tide flat. I heard the tires sloshing through mud and saw the water's edge appear in front of the hood. Bishop held up his fist. I stopped and stepped out into about a foot of water, just shy of the tail pipe.

"So what's the story with this scow?" he asked. "It is a scow, right? Or is it a Sharpie?"

"I don't know what to call it," I said. "My neighbor was building it. I think he just thought it up and did it, but he died before he got the hull done. The family gave it to me."

She was a low, narrow, box shaped sailboat about nineteen feet long and four feet wide with a profile that looked like a big smile. The main mast stood close to the bow and the mizzen was mounted right at the stern. Both were folded down on oversized wooden tabernacle hinges. Two leeboards, heavy six-foot-long ovals, hung from pivots on either side of the hull, resembling the shields of a Viking ship. The deck was bright white and the flat sides and bottom were a pristine maritime green. She sat in the trailer a good ten inches above the water.

"You built this thing?"

"Well, I put the skin on and finished the cabin. My neighbor started it, carved the masts and booms before he died."

"It's bad luck to paint a boat green you know."

I shrugged.

He looked at the white transom. "She got a name?"

"*Ursa Minor.*"

Bishop rolled his eyes. "Sorry I asked."

Harold appeared with a six-foot long pry bar that even he had to carry with both hands. Bishop didn't seem to be in a hurry. "Where'd you say you were going?"

"Around Devil's Head and up to Glencove."

He stared at me. "That's like ten minutes from here, Mac. You're talking about sailing all the way around the peninsula for twenty, twenty-five miles, easy. Why don't you just drive there and drag the sonbitch down the beach?"

"It's the maiden voyage. I'm going to moor it at a friend's place for the summer." Bishop waited. "It'll take a couple days," I added. Bishop still waited, but I said nothing else.

He detached the trailer from the ball then slid the pry bar sideways under the hitch, providing a lever on both sides. We lifted the bar and the trailer came up easily. We leaned into the bow of the boat to get the trailer wheels rolling. We kept pushing until water poured into our boots and crept up our thighs, then we lifted the pry bar and the boat slid off the trailer.

"Well, it floats," said Bishop. We dragged the trailer back up the beach and dropped the hitch onto the ball.

"You said Glencove?" he asked, pulling out a cigarette. "You don't mean Frank Roncevich's place?"

My friend Frank offered to let me raft up next to his old log boom tender moored in front of his place in Glencove. His family had lived there since 1910, but I was still surprised to hear Bishop say his name.

"Yeah, I know Roncevich," he said. "We played football in high school. Against each other, I mean," he added. "He used to be tough. You tell him I said that."

Harold walked up the beach hefting the pry bar in both arms. Bishop lit the cigarette, cupping both hands around the tip, then slogged after him in his wet clothes and boots full of water. "You're a hard worker, Mac." He climbed into the pickup with Harold and rumbled away.

I changed into a spare set of clothes and dropped my wet, fish stained shirt and pants into the parking lot dumpster. Half the day was gone by the time I'd secured my vehicle, climbed onto the boat, put up the masts, and got her drifting south. It was getting on to late afternoon before I started the outboard engine. It was small for this boat but quiet and adequate for flat water. There was no wind to speak of and the sun was warm and the receding tide carried us imperceptibly south while I dawdled in the cockpit and small cabin, trying to find new homes for all the gear.

I had a bottle of expensive bourbon with me, something I had promised my wife and my young son and myself I would not bring. I lodged it in a locker under my bunk, wedging it in place with a plastic box about the size of a thick book. The box contained my mother's ashes. I had not lived at home for some time because of these things, but I thought I might be able to return if I put them both to rest on this trip.

In another hour I had passed the mouth of Vaughn Bay, an ideal anchorage nearly walled in by a large sandspit. I had enjoyed many evenings there in an early settler's cabin, now grafted onto one of the large houses along the shore.

My host and I would sit outside in chairs built before the Indian War of 1855. We would nurse our drinks under the shadow of his ancestors buried in the hillside cemetery that overlooked their homestead.

It felt too close to my own home. I thought I might be spotted, maybe visited, invited ashore.

Further south, I found an anonymous notch in the shoreline under a few hundred feet of sandy bluffs topped with gnarled madronas. Their trunks tilted dangerously outward from the bluffs eroding beneath, but the sprawling branches continued to grow upward into a broad-leafed canopy. I dropped the anchor off the bow and paid out a hundred feet of chain and line. The mud bottom looked clear and close about eight or ten feet down. At high tide we'd be floating in twenty-five feet of water.

My head bothered me. There was something with my eyesight too. Sensitive but unfocused. I needed something to eat. I opened the locker with the bottle of bourbon and took it out. I put it on the bunk, thought it might slide off and smash, so moved it to the floorboards. I opened the galley locker and pulled out a can of macaroni and cheese. The gimbaled stove was stowed in the galley locker too. Setting it up would take time. I cut open the can and ate out of it. Then I took the bourbon with me up to the cockpit.

The sun was nearly gone but it wouldn't be dark for a long while. In high summer twilight stretches into hours. I watched the cliffs and beach, but they didn't move. It was slack water, the time between ebb and flood tide when there is little or no current, even on the eve of one of the biggest tides of the year. Water lapped slowly at the bow in a low

THE WOODPECKER MENACE

drum, drum, drum that rolled down the length of the wood hull. There was another sound too, of swishing or hissing though the evening was still. It came from a pair of crows or ravens flying with each other, at each other, tumbling, flapping high above the trees. I could hear the wind made by their wings.

I picked up the bottle and tore the seal off the top. The cork had a plastic cap that I started to twist. I meant to pour the bourbon over the side. The sound of the cork sliding against glass stopped me. There would be that scent. I held the bottle upright over the water remembering that smell and taste and let go.

It plunked down through the surface. But I knew I could reach over the side and pull it aboard when it floated back up. I could get a taste of smoky caramel and maybe saltwater after all. When the ripples from the small splash were gone, I could see through the green water to the bottle standing upright on the bottom, about ten feet away. One headlong dive could retrieve it. I looked over the side again after a few minutes of thinking, but the boat hadn't drifted any. The bottle was still there.

Movement caught my eye. The birds were much closer. They were crows. One broke away from the other, tumbling then soaring downward, the shape of a jagged arrowhead getting larger and larger. It flared its wings with a slap of air and landed on the short boom of the mizzenmast. I had never seen a crow that close. It took a tentative step on the furled sail, testing its footing. Large black eyes within a halo of blue or white stared at me from under a heavy brow.

"Hello," it said. It was a light voice, high-pitched like a crow's caw but sounding nothing like one. I didn't move.

It looked away and then back at me, nervously, I thought, as if fearing we might be overheard or that I didn't understand.

"Hello," it repeated.

"Hello," I said softly. The crow reared back and spread its wings. It nodded its beak up and down but still looked at me with both eyes. Then it stepped off the boom, flapped its wings, and disappeared into the trees.

* * *

There was a steady thumping on the hull the next morning. The cabin was half full of gray light. I thought we must be aground, or that a log had struck us. Topside the shoreline was barely visible in fog, a hundred yards further away than it had been the previous night at slack. The opposite horizon had disappeared. The thumping was just the same gentle lapping of water against the bow.

It was cold and damp in the cabin. I tried to keep my head still but felt a terrible electric jolt between my eyes whenever I glanced at something. I slowly pulled the gimbal stove out of the galley locker and screwed it into the receiver by the hatch, clamped a small pot to it, filled it with a pint of water, and lit up. I mixed coffee and sugar and canned milk into the hot water and sipped from the pot. After an hour, I could eat something.

The little engine pushed us slowly south through the channel between the peninsula and Herron Island, a private

tree-covered neighborhood served by its own small ferry. Beyond, the peninsula bends east as the mouth of Case Inlet opens at Dana Passage and Henderson Inlet before reaching the tip of the peninsula at Devil's Head. As we reached that bend the wind began to rise out of the south. I cut the engine and hauled up the small mizzen sail that extended behind the cockpit and then the big sail, a gaff-rigged main that ran from the mast at the front of the boat all the way to the end of the boom at the stern. It flapped around like a bird with a broken wing before snapping into place with a satisfying shudder, as if turning from canvas to steel.

The boat heeled over as it began to move under its own power, though I had to steer well off the wind to make headway. It would be a long day of tacking back and forth across the eye of the wind to get a decent angle and sail around Devil's Head. With the engine off there was only the water hissing by and the groan of lines under strain. The wind was cold and tasted strongly of salt. I was never one to get seasick but now the taste of the wind made me tremble.

I had timed this trip to ride the large outgoing ebb tide to the tip of the peninsula, but it was still flooding powerfully and the wind kicked up large waves. The hull shuddered whenever I hit one at a bad angle and a sheet of water shot up the sail and poured down across the deck and into the cockpit before draining away. I put a reef in both sails, making them smaller and reducing the boat's heel, and tacked southeast to southwest and back, making slow progress down the inlet. The shoreline disappeared once or twice when a squall blew by. Gray pillars reached down from the sky and rain shot against the sails and deck and me, bouncing like hailstones.

I was not queasy but I felt dizzy and weak. I managed to pull a can of beans from a locker below deck before everything turned white. I made it back to the cockpit and breathed deep. I hung onto the tiller and poured the beans into my mouth, then tossed the can half full over the side to avoid going below again. The electric jolts behind my eyes now tugged at my whole body in burning pulses that made me shudder. I would have stopped them with one long swallow out of that bottle left behind on the sea floor.

When I could at last look over my left shoulder and straight up the narrow passage between the point at Devil's Head and the large islands to the east, I pushed the tiller over and swung the boat around to the north, downwind, and eased the sheets to give the sails some room to fly. The pounding and rocking ceased once wind and current and boat and I were all headed in the same direction. The tide had a long way to fall, but the ebb current generated in these narrow channels flows powerfully north.

Devil's Head is undramatic in spite of its name. There is a steep bluff with a hazardous, rocky shoreline, but it is only on the chart, seen upside down, that it takes on a sinister profile with a sandbar brow and the thorny nose of land that is the lower end of Filucy Bay. I had thought it a fitting place to scatter my mother's ashes while under sail, but now wondered when I would ever be capable of doing that.

The width of the passage closed in from more than a mile at the southern opening to less than a quarter of that at the north end. The top of this bottleneck is nearly capped by the small cork of Pitt Island. Pitt looks something like a fortress with steep sand bluff walls and a heavily wooded keep surrounded by shoals and hidden obstacles. The shadow of a giant tree trunk passed beneath us, pointing upward and dark against the lighter gray of the water. Other sunken objects barely visible seemed to roam across our course. The narrow channel we followed passed within a few dozen yards of Pitt to the west, but the island remained out of reach. Indians had used it as a cemetery for centuries. They wrapped their dead in canoes suspended from trees to send them on their final journeys.

I recalled my own dead and how this sail was supposed to be her final journey. My mother's ashes had been sitting on a dresser in a hotel room next to unopened mail for months. She had died the previous winter after a decade spent orbiting the dark sun that is dementia. The strength of its gravity had torn everything to pieces. Memory, home, family. The wounded animal left at the end howled for my father, for her siblings, her parents, all long dead. But phantoms whispered back to her in voices beyond hearing, drawing her down pathways she was too frightened to describe. She lived in our home for years convinced that we who loved her better than our selves were simply other apparitions. She cast one long glance backward when that dark sun finally pulled her down, and the cornered animal recognized me. I was the one who had taken everything, she realized. Her house, her people, her body. I was the one who had robbed her, who had lied, who had let it happen. "It was you," she said, disappearing. "It was you."

When the shorelines moved apart beyond the island, I steered well to the west to avoid another dangerous shoal. The strange behavior of the opposing currents in this area conspired over time to create a broad mud plain that now lay out of sight but which emerged as an island once or twice a year on minus tides. Even skirting its edges I could see dark shapes beneath the surface, betraying its presence. There could be no question of going below deck to retrieve the ashes or of scattering them in this wind. It took enough effort to resist the pull of that black orb still aloft somewhere on my horizon.

Instead, I thought about my next drink. There would be something at Frank Roncevich's, at Glencove. He didn't know the purpose of this trip, only that I was arriving tonight. I hauled in on the sails, then let them loose, then hauled again, trying to coax more speed out of the boat. Past the shoal I was fighting the falling ebb, but Glencove was just six miles downwind.

By early evening I could see Frank's fire pit on the north side of the cove, and a big fire burning in it like a beacon. The wind had grown flukey and weak, and the gray lid above billowed and dissipated. The stillness rocked the boat, the booms swung at the end of limp sails. I hauled them down and started the engine.

Glencove is a winding, narrow bay protected by a sandspit and steep mud bank near the mouth. I slowed to a crawl to keep an eye on the channel. Broken tree branches floated all around. I smelled the rotting iron of seaweed covering the beach. Two or three trees along the shore had blown over and now extended a hundred feet or more into the bay. Frank's log boom tender, a flat work boat about thirty feet long with a small cabin, lay careened on one side above the high tide line, the floating dock still lashed to her side.

I killed the engine, tilted it out of the water, and coasted in. It was darker in the cove, but I could see people sitting around his fire looking in my direction. I hauled the leeboards and rudder up as the boat touched bottom, then jumped off and slogged to shore. I recognized Frank's lanky frame as he stood up and loped down to meet me.

"I can't believe you were out in this," he said. Frank was maybe twenty years older than me, though I'd never asked.

"In what?" I said.

"In this." He motioned with both hands to the water, the downed trees, to his tender high up on the beach.

"It didn't seem that bad."

"It was bad," he said. "I just hope we get another goddamn huge tide tonight to float my boat off. You'll be here for that." He headed back to the fire. "We're making hot dogs. You wanna drink?"

"Yes," I said. I followed him to the fire. He stopped abruptly and turned back toward me, pulling a folded piece of paper out of his flannel shirt pocket. "I forgot. Your wife stopped by." He held the note out to me. I took it and he walked away. On the outside was the word "Dad" written by my nine-year-old son. Inside, the writing was my wife's. "Please come back."

There was another man sitting on a log at the fire, nursing a coffee mug and a cigarette.

"Where you been, Mac?"

"Bishop. What're you doing?"

"Oh, the Bishop and I go way back," said Frank. He leaned over to pick up a kettle warming next to the fire and filled a mug, then picked up a bottle.

"That's good, just coffee for now." I said.

"Frank and I had business. Came over to discuss his boat." Bishop stressed the last word and craned his head around to look at the beached tender. "Guess it could make a nice cabin now."

"It'll float on the next tide," said Frank.

"It was that king tide today that did it, man. Big flood, low pressure, high wind. It's breaking up now though." Bishop looked at the darkening sky. "Higher pressure, lower tide, man. I think you're screwed."

"Well, if it doesn't float tonight, I'll get a bulldozer in here tomorrow."

"Oh, that's awful sloppy," said Bishop. "Not very nautical." He looked at me. "So how's your boat doin'?"

"Fine, held up fine."

"I need it tonight," he said.

The mug was halfway to my mouth. I stopped and looked at him. He appeared to have been working hard the last couple days and smelled strongly of tobacco and fish and saltwater. He slowly inhaled on his cigarette, nodding at me.

"What for?" I asked.

"Oh, Bishop's got a little errand tonight, a little business to take care of," said Frank. "I help out when he can't bother to get his own boat running."

"If I even had one anymore."

"Now whoever heard of a doctor who didn't own a boat?" said Frank. "Even an animal doctor. You should be disbarred." They laughed at this a little too much.

"So what's the errand?"

"Oh, it's a little maintenance job, really," said Bishop.

"Yeah," said Frank. "A little, uh, what shall we call it, maintenance, to, uh, a navigational aid?"

"Yeah," said Bishop. "It's annual maintenance. It's a local thing I do. Frank helps out sometimes, but, um." He nodded to the beached tender.

"So what is it?" I asked.

Bishop looked at Frank. Frank put his elbows on his knees and his hands together and looked into the fire. "It's something," he said. "When Bishop showed up I told him, 'Look, I'm out this year, but I've got this friend due in any time.' Turns out he already knew that. He just wanted to know if you could help out. I told him you could."

I was tired and didn't want to leave the fire. I could feel that pain shooting through me. I wanted some of what was in that bottle poured into my coffee mug.

"Yeah, I'll help."

* * *

Bishop stood on the bow leaning back against the mast, visible only by the glow of his cigarettes as he lit one after another. He would hold one out at arm's length, left or right, and I would turn the boat that way. He had stepped aboard, dropped a canvas bag with a few tools, and said nothing since shoving off.

The engine pushed us south with the last of the ebb, back the way I had come. The wind had disappeared and taken the clouds with it. A canopy of bright stars hung down to the shadows of land around us, all darker than the surface of the water at night. I could make out the faint light of the real *Ursa Minor*, the little bear, forever pursuing *Polaris*, the North Star, at the end of his tail. There was a dog barking somewhere ashore, a screen door slapping closed, the voices of people far away. Harbor seals surfaced around us, invisible, shyly rising and exhaling with a dull snort. A swirl of glowing plankton lit up their trails to the bottom.

Bishop's cigarette rose up and down in an arc. I throttled the engine down to idle, and he came shuffling back to the cockpit, one hand on the boom for balance.

"We're close," he said. "Take a look."

He put a hand on my shoulder and motioned over the side. I was startled to see the bottom just a few feet below the hull, glowing slightly from the plankton agitated by our bow wave.

We slid to a stop on the same submerged shoal I had edged past on a higher tide hours before. Now it was an island. Bishop picked up his bag and we slipped over the side. He held a small flashlight nearly straight down, illuminating only the mud in front of us. We stepped around seaweed, masses of barnacles, and starfish the size of platters, circling our way around to the center. Ahead, against the glow of lights from shore, I saw the shape of some animal hauled out on the mud. Another electric jolt went through me. I now recognized it as fear.

"Bishop," I said.

"It's all right."

We approached from behind. It looked like a large sea lion sitting back on its haunches and it had a thick mane of fur on its back. Bishop grabbed a handful and tore it off. I expected the animal to leap forward and roar, but it was just a large stone draped in seaweed.

"Hold this, will you?" He handed me the flashlight. The front of the stone, where the animal's head would be, was flat and faced north, the way we had come in the boat. It was a big piece of granite that must have been dropped by a retreating glacier many millennia past. Bishop bent down on one knee and tore off seaweed that had sprouted on its brow and face, revealing a mass of mussels and limpets and chitons. He started at the top of the stone, popping these off with a wooden chisel and club.

"There's more tools in there, Mac," he said.

I fished around in the bag for another chisel and club. When I looked up at the stone, a pair of eyes stared back at me. I felt another jolt. They were large dark holes carved within circles under a heavy brow that came down to a sharp point between, like a nose, or beak. Bishop continued to scrape algae beneath the eyes, knocking off sea life without harming the stone. There was more carving beyond.

"Can you believe how much crap grows on this thing in a year?" he said.

"How long has this been here?"

"Forever, Mac. It goes all the way down, right to the beginning." He scooped a few inches of mud out along the base, beneath a line of marine growth. I could see carved shapes running the width of the stone down into the mud.

"My gramma first brought me out here with a bunch of us back in '73. Somebody was trying to take this. Sonbitches had a friggin' barge out here with a backhoe. They'd already dug twenty feet down but the stone just kept getting deeper and wider the more they dug. It's carved all the way down. Gramma convinced them to go. Of course, she was well armed. She's the one gave me my job."

"Your job?"

"I come out once, twice a year, when we get a big minus like this. Make sure the eyes can see."

"How could these carvings extend twenty feet below sea level?"

"The sea wasn't always here, Mac."

We tapped away at the stone until it was clear of debris down to the mud. It was a spinning sky of faces and animals and shapes between. I could see bear and salmon and winged figures looming over human forms with limbs extended in greeting or warning or fear. There were waves and spirals and shapes I couldn't name swirling toward the top of the stone, whirling upward like the smoke of many fires, floating up to the large pair of eyes above.

"I feel like I've seen these eyes before," I said.

"Have you? Well, then. Guess it wanted a closer look at you. Or maybe you needed a closer look at it?"

Bishop stood and put his tools in the bag. The flood tide was starting to creep in around the base of the stone.

"The eyes tell the story but they watch the story, too." He held his palms up and closed his own eyes for a moment. "Okay," he said, "Let's go back this way. I don't like being in the story more than I have to."

We returned the way we had come, circling far out of the stone's sight. But it would watch us as we floated back up the inlet on the flood. It would watch my mother's ashes pour through my hands onto the rising tide. It would see us back to the peninsula, and home.

Acknowledgements

Many people put their shoulders to the task of creating this book. Tweed Meyer heroically transformed my words into evocative images entirely her own. Marla Klipper took that hard work a step further with her excellent cover design. My publisher of signal impact, Jan Walker, taught me to respect her sharp eyes and fear her pink pen. Colleen and Frank Slater loaned their X-ray vision and deep knowledge of Key Pen lore to copyediting. Early readers did the ugly work of critiquing evolving stories: Many thanks to Luke Dempsey, Therese Souers, Liz Stein, Irene Torres. A singular thank you to a singular man, my good friend Adam Klugman for his unblinking insight and boundless patience. Thanks also to those *femmes vitale* who allowed their images to inspire some of Tweed's drawings: the indispensable Molly Duttry, the irrepressible Grace Nesbit, the irreplaceable Cynthia Wilkerson. Perpetual gratitude to those absent friends Gene Battell, poet provocateur extraordinaire, and Jim Andrews, my first fiction editor and all-around, all-weather top shelf pal. Gentlemen, we are keeping your chili warm. To my long-suffering family, forced to sail through so many storms with wax jammed in your ears, this book is for you.

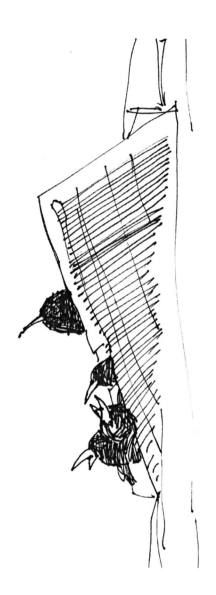

CPSIA information can be obtained at www.ICGtesting.com
Printed in the USA
BVOW020343080313

315012BV00001B/2/P